CAPTIVES
in a
Foreign Land

CAPTIVES
in a
Foreign Land

Susan Lowry Rardin

Houghton Mifflin Company
Boston

Grateful acknowledgment is given for permission to quote from "Black Water" by Patrick Simmons © 1974 WB MUSIC CORP. & LANSDOWNE MUSIC PUBLISHERS.

Library of Congress Cataloging in Publication Data

Rardin, Susan Lowry.
   Captives in a foreign land.

   Summary: Six young Americans are taken hostage and kept in a remote desert hideout by a band determined to stop the proliferation of nuclear weapons.
   [1. Terrorism—Fiction.   2. Antinuclear movement— Fiction]   I. Title.
   PZ7.R18144Cap   1984   [Fic]   84-12858
   ISBN 0-395-36216-4

Printed in the United States of America

S 10 9 8 7 6 5 4 3 2

To Jerry
   for adventure, sanctuary, joy

We are all
dangerous till our fears grow thoughtful.

— John Ciardi
"Incident"

CAPTIVES
in a
Foreign Land

One

The big jet slanted suddenly upward from the runway, banked steeply in the late afternoon sun, and headed northeast toward New York City. Matthew Vereen pinched his eyes shut against the sudden faceful of sunlight and the queasiness of the turn, until his brother rapped him sharply on the forearm.

"Come on, man, look at this tilt. You can look right out the windows on the other side and see the ground. Too bad we're not over the city. I'd like to see the Washington Monument from up here." Turned away from his own window, Matt's older brother Gilbert leaned heavily across him to get the full view.

"Hey, move it, Gib," said Matt. "Or I'll throw up all over you. Those steep turns really get to me."

"Well, you'll have some more to go through at New York." Gilbert sat back, bumping his long legs into the seat in front of him.

Their mother peered around at them. "Gib, will you warn me when you're going to attack like that? I deserve a chance at self-defense."

"Oh, sorry. Sure. I'll send you a telegram next time."

Matt glanced again at his mother, but she had already resumed her conversation with his father. It was amazing, the flip remarks Gib could get away with.

Gib yawned. "Don't worry, world. Once we get to Rome, I'll be out of everyone's way." He shot a quick look at Matt. "No doubt you'll be trotting around behind Dad playing senator's sheep dog, and I'll be free to prowl on my own."

"Don't count on it. Dad wants both of us to take the tours they've got for the families of delegates."

Gib groaned. "Oh, beautiful. Well, let me tell you, I'm not going to spend two weeks in Rome on somebody's leash. I'll find myself some decent excitement, one way or another."

A heavyset man came down the aisle, spotting members of their group and distributing something. He paused beside the boys' parents. "Afternoon, Senator, Mrs. Vereen. Certainly glad to have you with us. Can't be much of a treat for you, though. The minute the Senate goes into recess, you head off to a disarmament conference. What can you do with him, Mrs. Vereen?"

Matt's mother laughed. "As long as it means a family vacation in Rome, I'm not complaining."

Their visitor straightened. "Seriously, Senator, all of us academics are delighted to have you and the congressmen along. The symposium deserves to have impact on Capitol Hill."

"I'm looking forward to it, Dan. What's that you're passing out? Tickets to the Circus Maximus?"

"Ha! No, identification badges. To help keep the Washington delegation together when we get to Rome. There are nearly fifty of us, including the kids."

Matt looked at the pale blue sticker with NATIONAL CAPITAL AREA ACADEMY OF INTERNATIONAL AFFAIRS printed at the top. "Should we write our names on them?" he asked.

"That's not necessary. In fact, for your dad in particular, maybe not advisable."

2

"Security reasons?" Matt's mother asked.

The heavy man did not quite nod. "Just my unprofessional opinion, of course. No aides with you, Senator?"

Matt's father chuckled. "This is a vacation, remember? Besides, my boys can be my aides. Matt here could quote all my position papers. Flattering to his old man."

Their visitor smiled and lifted a hand. "Gotta get all my cattle branded before the New York group joins us. See you later."

When he had gone, Gib unbuckled his seat belt. "I'm gonna snoop around. Move your big feet, Vereen." He stepped past Matt, brushing against the magazines in his lap. "And gee, gosh, don't let me scatter all those *position papers.*"

"All right, Vereen," Matt growled back. "Get off my case."

Alone, he leaned back, watching through half-closed eyes as his father reached up to adjust the fresh-air nozzle. The group leader was concerned about the senator's safety. What if right now there were some crazy person on the plane, with a gun, eager to make headlines? "No aides, Senator?"

But danger was unlikely. And his father had said *he* could be an aide! Warming with the thought, Matt pulled out his wallet and unfolded a well-worn newspaper clipping. At the top of it was a large picture of him and his father in the senator's office in Washington, leaning against his father's big desk. They were looking at some papers together.

VEREEN CREDITS SON IN FREEZE DECISION

Last week U.S. Senator Martin Vereen announced from Washington, D.C., his support of a U.S. initiative to the Soviet Union for a mutual freeze in the testing, production, and deployment of nuclear weapons. Today, during a visit to his home office here in Ashton, Vereen credited his fifteen-year-old son, Matthew, with helping him decide to take this position.

3

"I wanted more research on whether the Russians would really accept a freeze now," the senator explained. "Matt has a keen interest in nuclear issues and volunteered. He spent a week of his summer vacation in the Library of Congress studying recent Soviet statements and came up with a lot of persuasive material. It was his work that convinced me."

Gib suddenly appeared, loping down the aisle with his bouncing stride. Matt quickly put the clipping away and leaned back once more, eyes closed, until his brother arrived. "So, what did you dig up?"

Gib brushed past him and flopped into his own seat. "One stewardess with no sense of humor. One group of people from India or somewhere, dressed up in sheets. A sum total of two teenage girls on the plane. Sitting way up front."

"One for you and one for me?"

"Negative. I'm not *that* hard up. You might be, of course. Go check 'em out."

It irritated Matt that he could never think of a wisecrack to throw back. He faked a yawn. "I'd rather sleep."

"Why not? After all, you have to get your rest if you're going to be the senator's head honcho in Rome."

"Shut up, Gib." Matt hunched sideways into a more comfortable position, with his back to his brother.

"Oh, well," Gib answered, cheerfully enough, "shut up yourself." He leaned down to dig a paperback out of his canvas bag.

Martin Vereen finished his briefing report and put it away. Beside him Paula sat with her head back, the newspaper still spread in her lap.

"Kids asleep?" he asked.

4

She turned to see. "Matt, maybe. Gib's reading."

"Gib went off to meet people right away, didn't he? That kid is so sure-footed and outgoing. I wish Matt had more of that."

"Why? Matt's not short on confidence, Martin. He just likes to observe things for a while before he jumps into them."

"He's going to need some independence, too, if —"

"If what?"

He didn't answer; he wasn't sure what he had started to say. "He's a special kid. Kind of . . . unfinished. It's like he's waiting to find out who he's going to be. With Gib, you can tell; with Matt, you can't. But he's going to be very interesting to watch."

"Martin, let him be ordinary. You make too much fuss over him. Like that nuclear freeze research. Oh, I know his material was good. But if it had been anybody else, even if it had been Gib, you wouldn't have made such a big deal about giving credit."

"If it had been Gib, I'd have fallen off my chair. He's about as interested in public issues as he is in chamber music." He had made her laugh; he grinned back at her.

Suddenly the full delight of their situation hit him, and he stretched contentedly. "Two solid weeks. Let's do everything together. Let's read your newspaper together, right now. One last check on the poor old world's situation, while we're still stateside." He leaned against her to peer at the paper in her lap.

She pushed back playfully, but her smile was thoughtful. "Let's talk, instead. No world situation tonight, Martin. Let's forget you're a senator. For tonight, just be a tourist, taking his family to Rome."

* * *

5

When Steven Mahlon and his parents boarded the big plane in New York, Steven's stomach was bothering him. His father frowned across at his mother as he fixed Steven's seat belt. "I sure hope we're not taking him to Rome *sick*. Who knows what kind of medical help we'd get over there? I told you a seven-year-old is too young to travel."

His mother's touch was warm on Steven's forehead. "I think it's just nerves. We're *all* excited, honey. You'll feel better soon."

And he did feel better, as soon as the plane was in the air. His father told him that many of the passengers were other teachers, going to the same meeting in Rome. One man — who looked disappointingly ordinary — was a real U.S. senator. There were some other children aboard, but Steven didn't see anyone else as young as he.

After a while the flight attendants brought dinner. It was fun to open the little containers of food, but Steven didn't feel like eating much. The stewardess who collected his tray commented on it. "He has a delicate stomach," his father explained.

"He'll be all right," his mother said.

The plane rushed smoothly eastward over the Atlantic as though it were racing to reach the night. Steven watched the red light in the sky fade and finally disappear. His parents turned on little overhead lamps that dropped tidy lapfuls of light for reading. That was nice; as long as they were reading he did not have to worry about what they were thinking. He loved being in the dark like that, with his parents on either side, held safe in their own separate worlds by the little reading lights, but leaving him free in the dark between them — free to escape to his secret thoughts.

His mother was smoking; spirals of smoke rose through the intensity of her reading light. Because of her they had taken these seats in the smoking section of the plane. After a while his father gave a tiny cough against his fist, and Steven felt a little twist of sadness in his stomach — the little twist that came whenever a bad time was starting. Tonight it would be the smoke. But perhaps it needn't be; perhaps he should seem to be asleep. After all, smoke couldn't bother him if he were asleep. On the other hand, if they thought he was asleep, they would be freer to argue . . . He couldn't decide what to do.

His father coughed again. Without looking up from her book, his mother said, "You two can sit up front. I've said that before."

"I'm not complaining." His father's voice was as hushed as hers. Their arguments were seldom loud.

"You were about to start hinting. I just thought I'd beat you to it."

"I can stand the smoke. It just isn't good for him, that's all."

"He's not the one making polite little coughs. Still, take him up front, if you like. There are empty seats."

"A family should sit together."

Now his mother lowered her book and the poison was in her voice, though it was still soft. "Wonderful. The classic double bind. So the only solution is for me to straighten up and quit smoking. Sorry, Richard. It's one of the few comforts I can depend on." This time the argument had come so far, so quickly. Steven wiggled a bit to let them know he was awake.

But now his father was too angry to care. "Your straightening up is more than I waste time hoping for. Smoking is the least of it."

His mother put her hand across her face; the cigarette trembled between her fingers. With the other hand she reached up and turned off her light. Steven looked around desperately. On the floor near him sat his mother's purse, with her thin suede gloves tucked into a flap. He leaned forward to pull one out and laid it across his knee. His parents were silent now, but the air between them seemed to crackle. Ignoring them determinedly, he worked with his mother's glove in the half-dark, flattening it out on his knee carefully so that each finger had its own definite space. Then he began to stroke it gently, steadily, smoothing the soft leather so not the tiniest wrinkle was left in it anywhere. Nice glove, he thought, focusing all his attention on it. Beautiful, soft glove. Rest, rest. Everything's all right.

From the corner of his eye he saw his mother reach for her handkerchief. He did not interrupt his quiet work. After a long time he began to hear a natural rhythm in her breathing.

A little later he sensed a change from his father's side, too. The bad time was over, for now. When he was sure, he tucked the glove back into place and yawned with sudden exhaustion. "Time for sleep, old man," his father said, turning out his own light and fixing Steven's seat so it reclined. His mother tucked a little pillow beside his head and smoothed his hair.

"G'night," he said into the dark.

"Sleep well, honey." His mother's voice was the last thing he heard as he slid into sleep, leaving his parents' truce in effect as the plane rushed into the night, his own limp body a bridge between them.

To Matt, who had not slept on the plane, the next morning's arrival was little more than a blur. I should be alert for this, he thought; I'm in Italy. But he could only stumble along past immigration officials, past swirling crowds of people, to a group of buses hunched reassuringly at an outside curb. Of the ride into the city he retained only a vague impression of heat, dazzling light, traffic, and row after row of red-tiled roofs.

In the hotel lobby, pleasantly cool, a sign printed in several languages welcomed delegates to the International Symposium on Nuclear Arms Control. On a bench a young American child slept with his head in his mother's lap. A suede glove had dropped to the floor beside them; Matt picked it up for her. "Bed," moaned Gib, looking at the child enviously. "Where's bed?"

A porter led the four of them to their rooms. Matt fell onto a bed and tugged at his shoes. "Sleep for a while, you guys," his dad said from the door. "But we'll get you up later. We don't have many free afternoons to do things together, and this is one of them." Matt sank into sleep like a rock into water.

He woke, all too soon, to Gib's punch on his shoulder. "Come on, come on. Dad says we have to go sightseeing." Matt groaned. "I'm exhausted."

"No, you're not, you're *hungry*. It's two o'clock. Come on."

They ate lunch in the hotel dining room, where Matt's father distributed printed materials from a fat brown envelope. "Here's this week's schedule of activities for the families of delegates. Tomorrow you kids see some of *ancient* Rome. Mainly the Forum, then a drive to the Catacombs."

"What are the Catacombs?" asked Gib.

"Underground places where early Christians used to meet in secret. Wonderfully clammy and spooky."

Gib sniffed. "Bet it won't touch *Raiders of the Lost Ark*."

Matt folded his schedule. "I'd really like to go to the sym-

9

posium with you, Dad. There's a workshop on European peace movements —"

"Maybe later in the week, Matt. This is your first trip abroad. Take the young people's tours, these first few days."

"So where are we going right now?" Gib asked.

"To see a bit of the Vatican Museum, before closing time. Then Saint Peter's." The senator checked his watch. "Let's roll."

Their mother gestured toward his lapel. "There's no point in wearing those badges now, is there?"

"No." The senator pulled off his sticker. "Peel 'em, boys. Your mother thinks it's safer to travel incognito. Look, Paula, I'll even wear my shades. Now I'm Joe Blow, American tourist."

They rode in a taxi through the hot city streets, and Matt observed it all with growing delight: the driver's fearless weaving through traffic; the old buildings with wide stone steps and wrought-iron grillwork; the sudden fountains, where muscular stone creatures frolicked in the spray. Later they sat in the Sistine Chapel, looking up at Michelangelo's famous paintings on the ceiling. "The heart of the Renaissance," their mother explained. "Faith in God, yes; but great faith in human beings, too."

Matt gazed up at the figure of a young man slouching drowsily on an elbow. "*That* guy doesn't look too ready for action. Hey, I've seen that before."

"It's very famous. That's Adam, and there's God reaching out to bring him to life." Together they looked up at the powerful hand pointing toward Adam's drooping one.

Gib snorted. "Adam looks really wiped out. Serious case of jet lag, if you ask me. I'd say poor old God sure has his work cut out for him."

"Paula," said the senator, angling his thumb toward his sons, "do we know these clowns? Come on, let's go next door to Saint Peter's."

They emerged onto the stone pavement of a vast piazza. After the dark of the chapel they stood still, blinking in the golden light of late afternoon, squinting toward the awesome dome of the waiting cathedral.

Two

The next morning Matt stood with his family on the steps of the hotel, looking down at a string of small chartered buses in the process of loading. His mother consulted the printed schedule. "The buses are due back here by five o'clock. You'll have plenty of time to shower before dinner. We'll meet you back at the rooms by six or so."

An official with a clipboard looked up at them. "Come on, Matt," said Gib. "Let's get this field trip over with."

"Americans?" the official asked as they approached. "Ah, yes. The Vereen brothers. First bus, please."

They clambered aboard, among other young people carrying cameras and sightseeing literature. Soon a short, gray-haired man with a cap like a conductor's climbed up the steps. He smiled at them beneath round, gold-rimmed glasses. "Good morning, young friends. My name is Ernesto. I am your guide for today, and your driver. Everyone on this bus speaks English, yes? Good."

A small boy appeared at the top of the steps. Matt recognized him as the child who was sleeping in the lobby the day before. Today he was wearing shorts, with a sweatshirt tied around his waist. His mother spoke from the doorway. "Excuse me. Is Steven too young to go? He's only seven. They don't seem to have anything planned for *young* children."

The guide tipped his head appraisingly. "Well, to me he is exactly big enough. Hello, Steven. Stefano. Maybe you will have a big sister or brother here today." He turned to the others. "Who will be a big sister or brother to this small Stefano?"

An older girl with long, dark hair raised her hand. "He can come with me, if he wants."

"Good, excellent. What is your name, big sister?"

"Jessica."

"Stefano, this is your sister Jessica. Now, Steven's mother, you go have a fine day at lectures, and Steven will have a fine day seeing things older than he can imagine." The child sat down beside Jessica and nodded good-bye to his mother.

"All right, my friends. Now I will see if everyone is here." Ernesto read their names from his list, peering out over his glasses to learn faces. Matt checked around, too, to see who looked interesting. "Good. Twelve of us, and twelve lunches here to eat after the Forum. Now, please, all must stay together. There are two other buses of English speakers, but you must stay with this bus. Okay? Then here we go to the Forum."

The little bus nosed abruptly out into the main flow of traffic. The morning was already hot, and the sudden flow of air through the open windows was welcome. At the front of the bus, Jessica captured her hair from the breeze and tied it behind her head with a silky green scarf.

Using a hand-held microphone, Ernesto explained what they were passing. "The shining white building ahead is the monument to King Vittorio Emanuele the Second. You can see him on his horse, up there in the center. Some people call this great white monument 'the wedding cake.' "

Gib laughed. "Hey, man, there's the only horse in history

to get stuck in icing." There was a chorus of soft snickers and heads turned, including Jessica's. Matt felt a familiar throb of envy.

When they got to the Forum, Ernesto pulled the small bus into place beside a string of big ones. "Now everyone please stay together. There will be many tourist groups here."

"Shall we leave our jackets in the bus?" asked a girl with a British accent. Matt noticed how the last part of her question curled downward instead of up.

"No, please. Take everything with you. Welcome, everyone, to the Forum of imperial Rome, two thousand years old and buried twenty feet deep in dirt until just the last century . . ."

Ernesto led them into the Forum, beside the low walls of ruined buildings, pausing often to gesture them closer with a hand held high. "These granite columns were part of the Temple of Saturn . . ."

They made their way along, past other tour groups clustered around hoarse-voiced guides speaking languages Matt couldn't identify. "We are now near the center of the Forum. Here Julius Caesar sat in power over his empire, and then was killed by a friend. Here Mark Antony gave the speech praising Caesar that started a war of revenge . . ."

He was a storyteller, all right; Matt could see the others catching his enthusiasm. Before they moved on, Gib had to jump up onto a wall and recite a few lines of the "Friends, Romans, countrymen" speech, rocking on his heels nonchalantly and using his Bogart voice.

Jessica was standing near Matt. "He's not bad," she said. "You're his brother, aren't you? Are you a comedian, too?"

Matt shook his head. "I figure one per family is enough." Couldn't he be more clever than that? "*At least* enough." She glanced back at him, and grinned.

14

Next, a younger girl in blue jeans climbed onto a pedestal of the vestal virgins to pose for photographs. A stocky kid with white-blond hair, she stood with her eyes raised soulfully and her fingers laced beneath her chin. "Ho, Martha," Ernesto called. "We hire you as a perfect vestal virgin. What salary do you require?"

Martha jumped down. "Hey, I'm easy. You can pay me in Oreos." Everyone laughed. Maybe this group would have fun together, Matt thought.

Near the end of the Forum Ernesto raised his hand at the foot of a huge arch. "Soon we will see the Colosseum, the stadium of ancient Rome. Then we will return to our bus. But first you must see this Arch of Titus, built to celebrate the victory over Jerusalem in seventy A.D. Inside you can see carvings of that story."

"I won't go in there." Everyone turned. The speaker was a boy several years younger than Matt, who hadn't said much before. "I'm Jewish. My dad told me Jews won't walk under that arch. That victory was a terrible thing. See that carving? That's Roman soldiers carrying off our holy candlesticks, stolen from the Temple before they destroyed it." Dark hair fell across the boy's eyes, and he pushed it back.

"You are Sidney, yes?" Ernesto nodded soberly. "You are right, Sidney. For Jews, for all people, this is a somber place."

"And your Colosseum." The boy pointed at the wall rising high beyond the Forum. "My dad says that was built by Jews brought from Jerusalem as slaves. When it was finished, they were killed."

"That is true. It is quite terrible. There is much to admire about ancient Rome — and much, much that was terrible. You will hear more of that when we get to the Colosseum, where many of *my* people, too — Christians — were killed." Ernesto looked around at the others. "Those who wish, walk

15

through the arch and see the carvings. Sidney and I will stand outside and keep faith with the dead."

Steven was glad they did not spend long in the Colosseum. The sun was overhead now, and the hot glare soon made even the big kids ready to head for the bus. Steven walked with Jessica. Some gravel had gotten into his shoe, and he limped. Jessica suggested he stop to shake it out, but he was too eager now for the shade of the bus. The Colosseum had been okay; the best thing had been counting all the stray cats he had seen there.

"Are you hungry?" Jessica shook her dark hair loose and then retied the green scarf around it. "I'm starved."

He shook his head. "I'm just tired of walking."

She laughed. "Stones in your shoe can't help."

She was wearing sandals. He thought her tanned feet looked very nice, walking beside his own smaller sneakers. "You're lucky. You can shake stuff out of your shoes easily."

"Of course. I planned it that way." She laughed again, as though happy about the day, about visiting Rome.

When they reached the bus he took a seat just behind her. He fished the pebbles out of his shoe and studied them, then tucked them into his pocket as a souvenir.

Ernesto was last onto the bus. "Are we all here? Who will count to twelve for me?" Several voices agreed on the total. "Good. Now we will drive out of Rome toward the Catacombs on a very ancient road, the Appian Way. On the way we will stop to eat our picnic lunch. Let's go, bus."

The engine churned. Jessica turned to smile at Steven. Then the bus moved, cooler air brushed past his face, and the patterns of light and shade around him began to dance. He thought of his parents back in the strange city, and clasped

16

his hands together in a secret ritual meant to help keep the two of them safe, and together. Then, with his hands still folded in his lap, he leaned against the window frame and fell asleep, remembering cats.

Matt hoped it was nearly lunchtime. Sure enough, soon after they had left the city, Ernesto turned off the main road and drove along a narrow drive, which ended in a parking area. On both sides of the bus stretched shaded slopes of grass. "Everyone please take a lunch bag and find a nice place to eat," Ernesto directed. "When you have eaten, please put all your papers in the rubbish cans. We can have half an hour here." Matt strolled over to join Gib under a tree.

Lunch turned out to be sliced meat in big rolls, apples, pieces of a flat cake with nuts on top, and bottled lemon drink. When they had finished, they stretched out on the grass and dozed for a while. Finally Gib yawned contentedly and sat up. "Ah. For a day or two, I can stand this all right."

Matt grunted lazily. "I suppose. But I'd rather —"

"But you'd rather be at the symposium! You turkey." Gib laughed abruptly. "Who but you would sit out here on a gorgeous day and wish you were inside listening to speeches and playing 'Son of Senator'?"

Matt couldn't let that go by. "Hey, knock it off. I happen to be really interested in that stuff."

Gib turned on him with a sharp glare. "Is that what you think? Is that seriously what you think? Then you've fooled yourself as well as some other people."

Matt sat up, angry. "What the hell are you talking about? What do you know about what I think?"

But now Ernesto was standing near the bus, clapping his hands. "Come, everyone. The Catacombs are waiting!"

17

Gib stood up and brushed off the seat of his jeans. "Forget it."

"Forget it, nothing. What're you getting at?"

"I said, forget it." Gib started off toward the bus. "Just try looking deeper into your own head, someday."

Damn. Gib did that, sometimes — make things go sour, all of a sudden, and then walk off before anything was resolved. Matt walked slowly back to the bus, angrily kicking a stone.

On board, he sat down next to the boy who had protested at the Arch of Titus. Sidney. They exchanged a nod. Ernesto climbed into the driver's seat. "Next stop, the Catacombs."

The bus started back along the narrow drive. Matt slouched low, staring at the back of Gib's head, half wishing he had a paper clip and a rubber band. Suddenly Ernesto slammed on the brakes, throwing everyone forward. "I apologize, my friends! Everybody is okay? We have a little trouble ahead. Please stay in your seats." He opened the door and climbed down.

"What is it?" someone asked.

Gib was sitting near the front. "Some guy's fallen off his motorbike right in the path. Another guy is with him."

"Is he dead?"

"No, no. He's moving. But he's kind of twisted up and holding his leg."

In a moment Ernesto appeared long enough to explain. "A little accident. I think there is a broken leg. We will try to get the man into the bus and take him up the road to a police station. Please stay quiet." He left again.

Gib resumed his report. "The guy's getting up. He's okay as long as he doesn't step on that foot. Here they come."

Matt sat up straight to see better. Ernesto and a stranger struggled up the steps with the injured man, who shot one quick glance at the passengers as he came into view. Then he was out of Matt's sight again, eased down to sprawl across a seat. Ernesto turned and started back toward the driver's seat.

In one instant there was only Ernesto's squarish back. In the next, the two strangers rose from their seats in a terrible singleness of motion and grabbed Ernesto, pinning his arms roughly behind him. He cried out sharply, and his head jerked back. Behind Matt someone screamed. The injured man — no, not injured at all — snatched rope from under his shirt and began to tie the guide's hands behind him. The other, older man turned toward the passengers; the short black barrel of a handgun emerged from his raised fist. Matt's heart pounded in his throat. Oh, God, no.

Suddenly a third man rushed up the steps, this one wearing a ski mask and carrying a pistol. At a word from the leader he pushed toward the back of the bus. Instinctively, Matt leaned out of the man's way, smelling his sweat as he passed. Ernesto began to shout. The leader struck him hard across the mouth and barked at him in furious Italian. The guide's glasses fell to the floor, and the gunman stamped on them with a sickening crunch. By now several children were sobbing in terror.

The man who had faked injury slid into the driver's seat, and the bus moved forward. The leader jerked Ernesto's arm fiercely and issued a torrent of instructions. The two of them knelt in the aisle, facing the rear. Struggling to keep his balance as the bus lurched back into traffic, heading away from Rome, Ernesto lifted his white face. "My friends, be calm. We've been tricked, but we'll stay calm, we'll use our heads, yes?" His captor smacked his arm and spoke again. "I will translate for him, and we will all do what he says. He says the older boys — you, and you, and you" — he tipped his head to Matt, Gib, and someone farther back — "are to sit down on the floor, in the aisle. Do not be afraid. Move slowly. Please move now."

From his seat in front, Gib turned and caught Matt's eye. They slipped slowly to the floor. At least Matt could still move; but his legs were shaking. Now, suddenly, he wondered: What is it they want?

"The man says, boys on the floor, please keep your hands around your knees where he can see them, so he knows you won't make trouble. Everyone else must keep your face this way, and your hands in your lap. No one is to look toward the window. Anyone who does will be hurt and tied up. If you want to lie down on the seat, you may — but keep your hands still and where they can be seen. Then no one will be hurt. Do what he says, my friends. Whatever happens, *whatever happens*, be still and give no reason for shooting." The leader's heavy eyebrows moved lower in suspicion, and he tapped Ernesto's arm to silence him.

Most of the passengers were quiet now, though there was still some soft sobbing. Matt's shaking was worse, and he leaned against a seat for support. Maybe this was happening because of Ernesto. Maybe he belonged to a different political party, and these were radical terrorists trying to prove their power. It didn't seem likely that it was just the *bus* they wanted . . . The more he worked at the question, the more it frightened him.

Eventually the bus began to slow, and the sounds of traffic intensified. A big intersection, Matt thought. The spokesman muttered to Ernesto, who said softly, "Everyone be very good now."

The bus paused, then started into a left turn. Everyone swayed to the right with the motion. But suddenly Ernesto was rising toward the left, swinging around so his shoulder smashed into the leader, bringing his knee up hard under the hand with the gun, then lunging beyond toward the driver. His tied hands useless behind his back, he threw himself forward against the steering wheel. For a moment the bus veered wildly, and Matt fell sideways. Then the leader grabbed Ernesto by the collar, shoved him back down onto his knees, and smashed his face against the metal side of a seat.

Passengers screamed. Ernesto fell forward onto Gib. Purple with rage, the gunman knelt on the guide's ankles and called out to the driver. Under control once again, the bus sped off in its new direction.

Ernesto had tried to make them crash, and now they had killed him. Matt would never forget that savage blow.

But no, Ernesto wasn't dead; Matt heard him groan. Gib, cradling the guide's head, looked up at the leader. "Hey," he said, "he's bleeding badly. We've got to do something." He doesn't speak English, you idiot, Matt thought, but his heart lurched with envy for his brother's courage. The gunman spat an angry word at Gib and began to tie Ernesto's ankles.

Gib's voice seemed to calm the other passengers. The sobbing quieted. Now Jessica spoke to the leader, using gestures to translate her meaning. "Let me put a bandage on him. Look, I'll tie it with this scarf. Who has something we can use? Oh, that shirt." She pointed to a boy across the aisle. "Can we use that?"

The answer, after a pause, was the slightest sideways motion of the gun barrel.

Jessica turned toward the boy. "Could I have your T-shirt?" He pulled it over his head. "It's sweaty," he said.

"That's okay." Kneeling, she folded the shirt into a pad and set to work. Soon Matt heard Ernesto's voice, answering hers.

The leader had turned to the driver. For the first time Matt noticed that when these two conversed, it was in a different language. The words were somehow simpler and more distinct, with clear consonants; they did not rush together with the liquid sound of Italian.

He became aware of rapid breathing beside him. From the corner of his eye he could see Sidney easing himself slightly lower in his seat. While the gunman still spoke to the driver, Sidney's right hand flew upward against his shirt and returned to his lap, holding a small, dark blue booklet. His passport. Several years younger than Matt, the boy was nevertheless carrying his own passport — which right now he seemed to be hiding, pushing it down into the crack between the seat and the wall. Why? Matt's mind was too sluggish with fear to imagine.

Gib and Jessica helped the guide back onto his knees. Jessica's green scarf was tied around his head, holding the homemade bandage against the wound on his forehead. His nose looked swollen and crooked, but what made the children gasp was the sight of so much blood. The top of his shirt was soaked with it.

"I am all right, young friends. Cuts on the head always bleed like a fountain of Rome. Now I am okay. Only now I, as well as you, must obey this man." The leader prompted him. "Remember — eyes always front. Hands in your lap, and still."

With his ankles as well as his hands tied, Ernesto had difficulty keeping his balance. Finally the gunman let him sit down and lean against a seat. He closed his eyes.

They rode for a while in silence. Matt tipped a wrist: it was just after two o'clock. Back at the symposium, afternoon lectures were under way. His father would act to rescue them — as soon as he learned what had happened. How long would that take? Had someone seen and reported any of the

22

trouble at the park or the big intersection? Or would it be dinnertime before everyone would realize the bus was missing? And how long after that would they begin to suspect a kidnaping?

Because — Matt could no longer avoid facing it — a kidnaping was what this nightmare must be.

Three

Once everything was quiet again and Steven was pretty sure Ernesto was not going to die, he lay down on the seat, carefully keeping his hands in front, and escaped into sleep. But he dreamed that there was blood instead of water pouring down over the stone horses of the Trevi Fountain, where he had stood with his parents the evening before. When he woke up, the first thing he was aware of was the sound of his own voice; he was crying.

He sat up, remembering everything, wondering whether it would be all right to wipe his face. He decided it was better not to move his hands so much, better to let the dampness dry by itself.

One thing had changed while he slept; the leader had switched places with the man in the mask, who now knelt near the driver and seemed to be giving him directions. They were far out in the country, racing through stretches of forest. Steven did not hear many cars.

Finally the bus slowed and turned onto a narrow, bumpy road. Beyond the front windows the trees seemed to tip crazily, left and then right. At last the driver paused at the edge of a clearing, and then moved on again, out of the shadows and into the hot afternoon sun.

Behind Steven the leader gave an order. Ski Mask untied Ernesto's ankles and helped him to his knees. The guide's face by now was badly swollen and dark with bruises; he was a terrifying sight. But his voice was calm as he translated: "Now we will stop. When we get out, move slowly and keep your hands down, where they can be seen. Bring jackets, but nothing else."

Suddenly there was a large shed in front of them. To Steven's surprise the bus moved directly toward it and into it, out of the sunlight into near darkness; the only light came from small windows high in the walls. Here were more men, waiting for them. For a moment he hoped wildly; were these Italian policemen, come to rescue them? No — they were greeting the driver. In fact, one man was wearing a ski mask, just like the first one's. Steven almost felt sorry for them; a hot August day must be a terrible time to have to wear a ski mask.

Ernesto was being led to the door. "Everybody come out now. Slowly, please, one at a time."

Steven's legs were shaking, but he stood up. The big boys sitting in the aisle got up stiffly. Jessica turned to look back at him — would they shoot her, even now, for turning her head?

The strangers waved them forward until they stood side by side across the dirt floor of the shed. One man just watched, arms folded. The boss, Steven thought. He had a short, very black mustache and a nose that arched high like the beak of a hawk. He spoke to Ernesto in strange-sounding English. "If you are weak, old man, you may sit down."

Ernesto answered briefly, shaking his head.

"Speak English; I do not know Italian. Now, you prisoners. You have seen what happens to one who disobeys. Do not make that mistake. We will now take the things you carry with you. Don't worry — all important things we will return to your parents."

Their things returned to their parents! Steven's heart dropped like a stone. He had seen a movie like that; it was what kidnapers did. He pinched his lips together to keep them from trembling. These men might kill him if he cried now. So he would not cry. This was not the first time he had kept from crying because that would have made things worse.

The Hawk was still speaking. "The boys will be searched. The girls must take out everything from their pockets. Now."

There were three girls. The younger two looked at Jessica. After a moment she reached into her skirt pocket, pulled out a wallet and a comb, and laid them on the floor. It frightened Steven to think these men would take all their private things. Would they take away their names, too? And all their deep secrets?

A man began taking the boys' watches and emptying their pockets. At his turn, Steven tried not to shrink from the man's touch; he must not insult him. The searcher's blue work shirt was wet under the arms as he felt all of Steven's pockets, finding only the pebbles from the Forum and the little snap purse his mother had given him. Inside was a thousand-lira note and a card with his name and the hotel phone number, for use in an emergency. This was an emergency, all right; and the little purse had done him no good at all. But it was his name they were taking, and her handwriting. Good-bye, he thought.

The searcher took everything to the Hawk. Now that Steven's eyes were used to the dim light, he could see better. At the crack between the big double doors, one Ski Mask was keeping watch, gun in hand. Parked beyond the bus was a small delivery truck. Against the opposite wall of the shed stood a few big dirty drums.

26

The Hawk looked up at Ernesto. "There are no passports here. Where are the passports?"

Ernesto shook his head. "Most parents keep their children's passports."

The Hawk turned to a boy. "Where is your passport?"

"My mum has it."

The Hawk's eyes narrowed. "Where is your home?"

"London."

He spun back toward Ernesto. "These are *Americans,* yes?"

There was a little pause before Ernesto answered. "Not all of them," he said finally.

"You are lying," the Hawk snapped. "We have researched. Your bus has the children of the Americans at the symposium."

"And children from other English-speaking countries, too."

The questioner stared at him, then barked at another man. Now all of the strangers were upset. Finally the Hawk turned back. "You are lying. These children are Americans. We know some names, and you — or they — will tell us the others."

Ernesto gazed back at him. "You can learn their names yourself," he said finally, sounding sad. "My passenger list is in the bus."

In a minute the Hawk returned, studying the list. "This list tells only six Americans. All of you! Tell me your names and your countries." He pointed. "You speak first."

"Gilbert Vereen, U.S.A." Steven looked down the row at the speaker and for the first time saw how Gib's shirt and jeans were soaked with Ernesto's blood. He gasped. To his relief, the Hawk ignored him.

"Matthew Vereen, U.S.A."

"Duncan Caldwell, Scotland."

"Edward Fisher, England."

"Martha Stediman, U.S.A." That was the chubby blond girl who had acted like a funny statue in the Forum.

"Frederick Bollinger, Canada."

"Margaret Fraser, England."

"Sidney Goodman, U.S.A."

It was Jessica's turn. "Jessica Portere, U.S.A."

Now his own. "Steven Mahlon, U.S.A."

And the last. "Brad Dobrowski, Canada."

The Hawk lowered the paper. "This list is right. But where is Callender? Where is Fineman?"

Again Ernesto shook his head. "I don't know. Maybe they were on one of the other buses." The Hawk frowned at him. "There were three buses of English-speakers, you know."

Once again, a burst of angry conversation among the captors. No, thought Steven; the Hawk *hadn't* known that.

Finally the Hawk turned back to the captives. "Now. Everyone sit. You will have water to drink, but you must be quick." Two big plastic bottles were brought forward. "I do not require you to drink, but you will be sorry later if you do not."

When the bottle came to Steven, Jessica said, "Drink lots, okay? We don't want to be thirsty later." Steven swallowed as much as he could. The water was warm.

The Hawk checked his watch. "When you have drunk, I suggest you go use the private place. There is no real toilet, but you can go into that corner, behind those drums. One at a time. This man will point who can go."

The guard motioned to Steven first. "Better go," Jessica whispered.

He stood up and headed toward the privacy of the drums. Walking off with everyone's eyes on him gave him a surprising surge of courage. He straightened his back. His bladder agreed with Jessica; this was a good idea. *You're full of good ideas,* he would say to the Hawk, if he dared. Sarcastically. *Boy, you're just full of good ideas, aren't you, buddy?*

But when he came back and saw all the white faces of the older children, the brave words flew from his head. Because now he would have to find out what was going to happen next.

Martin Vereen had not had a really good shave since leaving home. He took time with this one now, leaning forward over the wide porcelain washbasin. Paula rested on the bed, watching him.

"I covet that sink," she said. "We could put everything that's in our medicine cabinet along the back of that thing."

"Mmm." He lifted his chin for the blade.

"A nice dinner, and then early to bed; that's what I want."

"What about tomorrow? You want to come to sessions with me again, or are you ready for a break?"

"I'll go back with you. It was exciting today." She yawned — a contented little glissando. "And I stopped worrying about you. The atmosphere here is so positive. What a heady gathering! I began to believe the old world might make it."

He dried his face slowly, enjoying the nap of the towel. "These people sure keep me on my toes. I'd forgotten how much freer academics are to really *think.* I'll have culture shock, going back to the deadly old pieties on the Hill."

She lay back and stretched. "You know that woman who does the translating from Italian and French? Elaine Goodman. Her husband's a delegate, and they brought their son. They're really cosmopolitan — had a year here at the University of Rome and a couple of summers in Israel. We thought maybe the three boys might sightsee together. Sidney's only thirteen, but he speaks Italian, so they could get around on their own."

"Sounds good." He dug into the suitcase for socks. "Speaking of the boys — we'd better be sure they're back and bathing. We should go down in about twenty minutes."

"I'll check." She slipped on her dressing gown. Almost at once she was back. "There's no answer, and their door's still locked. It's after six, Martin. The bus *must* be back."

He slid into his shoes. "They're probably hanging around the lobby. I'll find them while you get dressed."

The sharp ring of the room phone made them both jump. "Senator? This is Perucci at the communications desk downstairs. Have you had any message this afternoon from your sons?"

"Why, no." He looked up. Paula was watching him.

"I mean not to alarm you, Senator, but their bus has not returned. We hope it has just had mechanical difficulties, but — the driver has not telephoned."

"I see. Have you notified the police?"

"Yes. They will be here immediately. But we have many worried parents down here already. Will you come down, please?"

"Of course. We'll be right there." He hung up and drew a deep breath to tell Paula.

The last of the captives were taking their turns behind the drums. Matt saw Gib eyeing the double doors where the guard was standing watch. What if he and Gib together rushed the man; could one of them possibly get out and away? But Gib did not turn to look at him, and of course it wouldn't have worked. There were too many men, with too many guns.

The Hawk spoke. "Everyone stand up. We will now tie your hands. See, we will tie them in front; that will be more comfortable for you." There was a murmur of fear as the pro-

30

cess began. "Silence, or I will not tell you what will happen! That's better.

"Some of you and your guide will stay here overnight, sleeping in your bus. You must be completely quiet. Guards will watch you from here in the shed, until dawn. Then they will leave you locked inside for a short time. Within two hours, the authorities of Rome will learn where you are waiting. You should be free by the middle of the morning."

Matt wanted desperately to believe that the man was telling the truth, and that he and Gib would be among this group. But at the moment his own hands were being tied in front of him, sickening new proof of powerlessness.

"The rest of you will ride farther. We must cover the mouths of these people, to be sure of silence. We leave at once." In what? For the first time Matt looked hard at a small green delivery truck parked beyond their bus.

Ernesto burst out in Italian and stepped forward. The Hawk snapped at him. "Stay still. And speak English, old man."

"If you are going to take some children away, take me, too. I can help them. They will be more content if I am there."

"Quiet, fool. You have already proved you cannot be trusted. You are lucky we do not kill you. Now — these people step out: you, you, you . . ." He pointed to Gib, then Matt, then others.

Matt's hope drained away in an instant. He looked at Gib, who was looking at Ernesto. Ernesto's face was twisted, and he trembled. Finally he said, "I cannot help, my friends; I cannot advise what to do. If you go, my blood goes with you."

"Move!"

Gib stepped forward. Matt and the others followed. The Americans, as Matt had feared. Beside him, his brother was being gagged. Then there were hands and a dirty cloth in front of his own face, and a pressure and a silence that terrified him. For a moment, he fought panic and nausea. He would vomit — vomit, choke on it, and die.

Ernesto was speaking again. "Speak louder, Stefano. What is it? Please, the boy wants to say something. Jessica, ask him."

The Hawk hesitated. Jessica explained in a shaky voice: "He's afraid to be gagged. He says he has asthma. If he has an attack with the gag on, he's afraid he'll die."

Now Ernesto was pleading. "Leave him behind. He's too young. With the asthma and the fright —"

"Silence! The boy goes. Boy, you may ride without the cloth if you are completely quiet. If you make noise, I myself will tie your mouth. Very tightly. Now, you others, get into the bus. Americans, over here to the truck."

Ernesto called across to them. "Courage, young friends. I will carry your love to your parents. God goes with you."

The inside of the truck was very dark. An ancient organic smell suggested it once had carried vegetables to market. This odor was tinged with a smell of dust, rising from what seemed to be gymnastic mats lining the walls and floor. Crouched at the front end of the truck and using a flashlight as a pointer, the Hawk ordered the captives to sit with their backs to the walls. Matt lowered himself awkwardly, his hands useless, his feet bumping other people's in the dark. Two guards climbed in last, pulled the doors shut, and moved thick panels of some kind to cover them. Camouflage, maybe; in case someone tried to look into the truck. And — soundproofing. *That* must be the reason for the mats, too. Matt snapped his head back sharply in the dark against the softness behind him, and heard only a faint thump.

The Hawk rapped against the cab wall and the truck started — backing slowly, turning, gathering speed. For some time they bumped over a rough lane; then there was another turn and they were off, much faster now, on a paved road.

32

In the pitch black of the truck, with his hands and mouth bound, Matt seemed to be at the dark core of nightmare. Gib was sitting beside him, but not close enough to touch; he could not even hear his brother's breathing. No sight, no human sound. How could he control his head, keep himself from panicking? He would concentrate on what must be happening in Rome. If the adults did not already know of the abduction, they would soon. Again and again he made himself imagine details of how the investigation might begin. The goal was steady thinking, steady breathing. With the gag over his mouth, natural breathing was doubly important.

After a while a beam of light made him open his eyes. The Hawk had turned on his flashlight again and was checking the prisoners: first the tied hands held useless in each lap, then the gag and the eyes above it. Across from Matt the beam of light caught Sidney, his dark hair down over his eyes but not quite hiding his frown of fear and outrage; then Jessica, her face still but her cheeks wet with tears; then Steven, his thin face white, his ungagged mouth open, breathing normally while he could, waiting for the asthma. Then, like a shock of cold water, the beam was in his own face, and he shut his eyes against it.

Who else was there? On this side himself, and Gib beside him. But there was a sixth person, sitting beyond Gib; yes, the fat little blond girl. Martha someone.

The Hawk snapped off his light and spoke, just loud enough to be heard over the creaks and jolts of the truck. "Good. So American children do not *all* behave like selfish babies. I congratulate you. If all goes as we have planned, you will be safely back with your families soon. I suggest you sleep now."

The tight rope around Matt's wrist had made his hands begin to throb. Perhaps he could use gravity to help the circulation. He raised his knees in front of him and propped his

33

hands against them. That did help; suddenly sleep seemed possible.

He dozed fitfully, waking whenever the flashlight made its rounds. The Hawk seemed to be keeping the light low, out of faces. No doubt it was in his own interest not to wake people. Still, it seemed like a courtesy, and Matt felt grateful, even after reminding himself fiercely that this must be how the psychology of slavery worked: thank you, master, thank you for not beating me anymore. Oddly, both the gratitude and the deeper integrity that resisted gratitude were reassuring to him. I'm still myself, he thought. He slipped into a sounder sleep.

Four

Matt was jerked awake by the sudden pitching of the truck, which had left the paved road and was creeping down a deeply rutted track. There were muffled groans in the dark as one wheel after another bumped down into a hole. Beside him Gib grunted into his gag. The rag across Matt's own mouth was damp with saliva.

The truck stopped. He sat in the silent dark, still sloshing with adrenaline from the sudden waking. After a moment there was a rap on the outside of the door, then the Hawk's voice, very soft: "Everyone awake now, and be ready to move. You will be absolutely quiet and do as you are commanded." Matt could see a widening crack as the doors were opened, then the first two hostages being pulled to their feet and led outside. Would there be any way to give an alarm here, or escape to get help?

The Hawk stood in the door. Listening, Matt suddenly recognized the soft rhythm of waves, and caught a whiff of salt water. The ocean! No, no, of course not — the Mediterranean.

Now a guard was pulling him up, holding him by the arm as he took the long step down to the ground, into a light drizzle. Through the mist in front of them stretched the sea, vast and dark. They hurried down toward several crude docks that reached out into the water. Matt's hope dissolved; there was no sign of life after all.

Beside the nearest dock waited the dark shape of a boat — a wide boat with a tall mast and a large outboard motor. It was open, except for a low, makeshift cabin in front of the mast, into which the prisoners were crawling. Matt could see Gib trying to pull his long legs in out of the rain.

Guards held his elbows as he slid down into the boat. Behind him came Sidney. Together they were pushed forward toward the low cabin, which was already crowded. "Lie down," hissed the Hawk.

Stumbling, Matt curled down against Gib until the bare ribs of the boat pressed up under his own and a cold ooze of oily water began to spread upward through his clothing. Behind him someone pulled a heavy tarp into place over the opening of the cabin. Pitch dark once again. There was the deep soft whir of an engine, and the boat was moving.

Again they were beyond hope of help, speeding away from land into increasingly rough water. Toward what? He was ready to cry with despair; and in fact he could hear soft sobbing deeper in the cabin. But the muffledness of the sound jerked his mind awake; it would be terrible to get a stuffed-up nose when you were gagged. To his relief, the noise soon stopped.

The water grew rougher by the minute. Again and again the boat slammed down on the flat back of a wave so viciously that he thought his ribs would break. From time to time a great jet of spray would slap down, and the tarp did little to keep him dry.

For the rest of that ride he could not even focus on the terror of what was happening. The battering of his body crowded out everything else. It seemed interminable.

Finally, the pitch of the engine decreased, and there were

36

new sounds: another engine, the slap of waves against something big that grew steadily closer, then a sudden shocking bump that threw him hard against Sidney. In a minute the tarp was pulled away, and he looked up: above him like a wall loomed the side of a huge yacht. The Hawk stooped to untie Sidney's wrists. "Now everyone will climb the ladder into the big boat."

When his own hands were free, he couldn't make them work. He was hoisted by a guard and moved on legs that had no feeling toward the ladder. Hands from above and below pulled and shoved him onto the yacht, where he was led down a staircase, along a narrow passageway, and into a large cabin.

The bright light hurt his eyes, but he gave a shuddering sigh of relief at the room's warmth and comfort. Cushioned benches lined the walls. Soon all the captives sat slumped back against soft pillows, blinking dazedly and rubbing numb hands. Crew members — new faces — removed their gags, and Matt passed the cold back of a hand across his raw lips.

The other five looked awful. Gib's gray face and sunken eyes were almost as ghastly as the great blooms of Ernesto's darkened blood on his shirt and jeans. Sidney sat shivering, his hair plastered against his forehead. Jessica had taken off her wet sandals and was flexing and straightening her legs. The youngest children — the wispy Steven and the more substantial Martha — lay back without moving, their ashen faces vacant with exhaustion. Matt suddenly realized with relief that Steven had not had an attack of asthma.

The Hawk and two other men appeared at the door. Both strangers were dark-skinned and wore long, loose robes. The taller of the two had heavy lines in his face and an aloofness that suggested authority. This one stood staring at Jessica and Martha, murmuring to the Hawk. At last he spoke to Jessica. "It is not our wish to take women prisoners. If your fathers had kept you in the protection of your homes, you two would not be here now."

Jessica leaned forward, brushing wildly tangled hair from her face. "Send us home, then."

The stern gaze did not change. "That is not possible. We accept what Allah wills. Your return depends on the response of your government to our just demands. If our demands are not met, the guilt of your blood will be upon them, not us."

Jessica had had the guts to speak to him; so could Matt. "What are your demands? It may take a little time, but I'm sure they can be met. If you want money —"

"Money!" The leader spat the word toward Matt's feet, his mouth curling in disdain. "We are not greedy Americans. You need know only that you are captives of those who serve Allah and his justice, against the blasphemous corruption of power." Matt sank back. Whatever these people wanted, they were clearly fanatics.

"Soon you will eat. Assad, here, will guard you. He will let you use the W.C. through that door, one at a time." The Arab turned and left the room. The Hawk followed.

"He means the washroom." The younger man's tone was different — teasing perhaps. He stood with his hands on his hips and his head thrown back. "The bathroom. The *powder* room." The accent was different, too; it sounded much more American. "There is a sink in there, and soap. You see, we are good hosts, even to prisoners." He turned away.

Matt moved closer to Gib. "Iranians?"

Gib shrugged.

Sidney whispered "It's Arabic they're speaking."

Gib looked at him. "What country?"

"I don't know. Careful, he's looking."

Once they had washed, they all looked better. Jessica and

Martha took turns smoothing each other's hair. Gib said, "Hey, Stefano, you've got crud from the bottom of the boat plastered to the back of your shirt. Come here and I'll pick it off."

A crew member brought food — oranges, flat rounds of bread, hot tea in plastic mugs. The tea was comforting; the bread was chewy and good. When they had eaten, the older Arab returned, carrying a cloth sack. From this he dug out things which Matt recognized; yes, there was his wallet.

"We know your names, and now we will learn more. You, there, are Gilbert Vereen. You are Matthew. Your father is Senator Martin Vereen. This is correct?"

Gib answered. "Yes."

"Ah!" Assad was staring from Gib to Matt, his face blazing with sudden excitement. He turned to whisper for a long moment to the older man, who listened gravely and nodded before continuing.

"You are Jessica Portere. Your father — no, your mother!" — he shook his head, frowning in disapproval — "is a representative from Massachusetts." Jessica nodded. "Sidney Goodman — is your father in Congress?" Sidney shook his head. "Speak. What is his work?"

"He teaches international relations."

"Your mother — what is her work?"

"She's a translator."

Their interrogator exhaled sharply. "Steven Mahlon. Your father is a congressman?"

"Um, I don't think so. He teaches about government. My mother works in a library."

"Martha Stediman. Your parents?"

"They teach history. My dad's at a college and my mother's at a high school."

"Your parents not in government at all, you three?" They

39

shook their heads. The leader's eyebrows jutted low over his face. "So, only half of you are children of legislators, and one of the three is a woman. Never mind." His eyes came back to Gib and Matt. "We will make the most of what we have." He selected the brothers' wallets and began to look through them.

So Martin Vereen was a target of all this. Why had mention of his name made Assad so excited? Shivering, Matt watched the Arab poke through his private things with bony fingers. He had found the newspaper clipping about Matt and his father. He took a long time with it. Finally he passed it to Assad and looked up at Matt. "So. This is true?"

"Yes."

"You persuaded your father to oppose the arms race."

"Well — I helped research facts for his decision."

"You are against your country's imperialist use of nuclear power?" Matt looked uneasily at Gib and the others, but saw no help in the white faces. "Answer."

"I don't agree with what you say about our policies. But I think we already have enough nuclear weapons. Making more doesn't do any good and uses up a lot of money we need for other things."

"So. You don't want more weapons because it uses up your money. Typical American thinking. Not because those weapons threaten millions of people who aren't even your enemies. Not because they violate the will of Allah, whom you claim to worship."

Out of the corner of his eye, Matt saw Sidney lean forward. "It's not the will of God for Russia to blow us up because we're not smart enough to defend ourselves!" Sidney's voice — still the higher voice of a child — was steely with defiance.

"Quiet! You will not speak unless I demand it. You will be

40

silenced with a cloth if you offend again." Creased in anger, the dark face was terrifying. Sidney was still, but he continued to stare back. Matt wiped sweat off his lip. If they weren't careful, that gutsy kid could get them all killed.

The Arab returned the things to the bag, stood up, and glared once more at Matt. "I have long known that U.S. policies are selfish and blasphemous, that Americans kneel to their money and not to their God. And I have heard that they scorn their old men, and make idols of their children. But I did not know until now that they rely on the counsel of those children in making policy. Perhaps that explains many things." At the door he turned back. "From now on you will all be under the watch of Assad. You will give him no trouble."

Matt drew a shaky breath. It was alarming, how the man could twist everything.

Assad stood with his hands on his hips, looking pleased that it was now his turn to be in charge. He walked toward Sidney, swaggering a little. "*You* are lucky he did not throw you to the sharks. Like *Jaws*." He made a flashing bite with his own brilliant teeth. Behind his sneer flickered a gleam of humor. "Yussef is an important man. You must show respect, even if you are ignorant Americans. You must show respect to me, too." Matt watched him closely. This Arab was different. If they worked carefully, they might learn things from him.

Gib might have been thinking the same thing. "Is Yussef the boss of all of this?" he asked.

Assad shook his head. "No, but he is the chief aide to our *za'im*, our 'boss.' "

"Who is that?"

"That is not your business; you will never see him. Nor are you to know where he is, or where you are going, either. Americans are completely ignorant of the Arab world, and we shall leave you that way." He dropped into an empty seat and leaned his head back to rest. But it was so clearly an act that Matt kept watching. He was showing off; he wanted them to admire him. In time they might find a way to use that.

Sure enough, Assad soon opened his eyes again. "But I will tell you that he is a very important za'im, the leader of a new, secret brotherhood that stretches across the whole of Islam, into many countries. We unite to preserve the world which Allah created, so that there will be human voices left to praise him. Our za'im is the one who has ordered your capture, and certain other actions. When your country responds to our demands, he will be the one who will say whether yes, the response is good, you can all go back to your families, or — no, the answer is no good."

"What would happen then?" The voice trembled only a little; it was Martha's.

Assad shrugged elaborately. "The za'im will decide." He frowned suddenly. "Now I am tired of your questions. It is the middle of the night. Sleep while you have soft cushions; it is not a luxurious American house you are going to." He called out, and a guard appeared at the door with a gun in hand.

Sidney began one more question. "How long till we —"

"Silence!" Suddenly Assad was roaring. "You, Sidney Goodman, you may yet be thrown to the sharks. You are not even a congressman's son; you are worth nothing to us. Do not make us angry again. Now all of you, sleep, and no talk. This man will see that you do as I say." He disappeared. The guard squatted on his heels and did not move again, except to blink his eyes.

Matt stretched out on the bench, moving carefully because of his bruised ribs, and thought of the shed, the bus, the tied prisoners waiting in it. The wounded Ernesto. How many hours till they would be found? And then, what could they tell that would help the search? The fear began to swell again. Dad, he thought, here we are. Churning through the Mediterranean toward — somewhere. Here come a million vibes to help you figure out where we are. Please, God, help my father find us.

Five

Martin Vereen was used to being at the center of public crises: used to ringing phones, the hurried arrivals of officials, the door shut against waiting flash bulbs and reporters' questions. What was new was having this external whirl matched by an inner chaos. Did it show in his eyes? He could see it in Paula's.

It was the worst night of their lives. At ten o'clock, when the Roman police acknowledged their suspicions of a kidnaping, diplomats representing the nations of the missing children were waked and notified. By midnight the American ambassador had called the U.S. Department of State and arrived at the emergency center set up in the hotel lounge. Martin, who knew him slightly, pumped him for information. "Do you think it's the Red Brigades?"

"Offhand, no, Martin. The logical connections aren't there."

"Someone from the outside? PLO extremists? Baader-Meinhof?"

The, ambassador shook his head. "Can't say for sure, of course. But nothing clicks."

Martin rubbed his face. "The possibility of this never occurred to me. We talked about *my* safety. My God."

Parents of the missing young people huddled in clusters,

or paced alone down the long room and the corridor beyond.

A stricken Elaine Goodman stood with Paula. "Ironic, isn't it? We hoped your boys and our Sidney would spend some time together!"

"Let me tell you, I've been feeling grateful for Sidney. Thank goodness one of the kids speaks Italian!"

Martin watched as a long-haired young woman holding a cigarette in a trembling hand approached the congresswoman from Massachusetts. "You're Jessica's mother, aren't you? My husband *said* Steven was too young to go. And he has asthma! But whenever I start to panic, I make myself think of your daughter. She said she'd look after him. That helps." She closed her eyes and tried to steady the quivering lids with long fingers. The other mother touched her arm. Martin turned away.

Throughout the night, investigators traced and retraced the probable route of the missing bus. It had last been seen as it left the Forum; it had never reached the Catacombs. Several picnic sites were scoured for clues, and at one the remains of the group's bag lunches were found in trash bins. Between there and the Catacombs, no clues were discovered.

In the hotel lounge, nothing basic seemed to change until midmorning. Then came a phone call that electrified the air. The translator explained aloud: "A local radio station has just telephoned police headquarters. They've received an anonymous message which may or may not be a hoax. The message is that as a political act some of the children have been taken to an undisclosed place of hiding, but that the others are to be found safe in the general area of Cassino, approximately eighty miles from here. Police have already been dispatched to investigate. Please stay calm; we do not yet know whether the message is genuine."

Martin's voice quelled the burst of excited response. "Has any organization claimed responsibility?"

The translator consulted the inspector. "A name was given, but we are not familiar with it. *Tawbah.* T-A-W-B-A-H. Patience, everyone, please. The story must be checked."

Paula turned to Martin. "Tawbah. What on earth is that?"

"I don't know. I think it might be an Arabic word."

"Arabic! Muslims, Martin?"

"I don't know."

An agonizing hour passed before verification came. There was silence in the room while the message was received, then translated: "Five children and the bus driver have been found, tied but unharmed — except for the driver, who has injuries of the face and head. The names of the children now safe in the hands of the police are Margaret Fraser, Brad Dobrowski, Edward Fisher, Duncan Caldwell, and Frederick Bollinger."

A gasp went through the gathering. The parents who now slumped with relief masked their reactions for the sake of those who stood still, devastated. Martin and Paula stood without touching. He thought: I have betrayed my children. I let them believe the world is safe enough to grow up in.

"The children are being brought to Santo Spirito Hospital for routine examination. Their parents will be driven there to wait for them. The other parents are asked to remain here. The authorities will give a complete briefing as soon as possible. Apparently the bus driver is very eager to talk to you, too, but first he must receive medical care."

Jessica's mother spoke in her warm, gravelly voice. "Has he given any clue to who the kidnapers are?"

A pause while the question was relayed. "He believes that most were not native Italians; that they were speaking Arabic."

46

A chorus of questions: How were the other children taken away? How were they being treated?

"I'm sorry, we have no more information yet."

Martin skirted the crowd to catch the ambassador. "So, it's the Americans they've taken. What are you going to do?"

"Call the White House at once. We'll have State get a team over here as fast as possible. At least now we can pull out all the stops. Look, will you organize the parents?"

"Sure."

"We'd better get full information on the kids — medical problems, anything we ought to be aware of. Get background on the parents, too, anything that could tie in with this — something they've been exposed to that's politically sensitive, national security issues, whatever. See if you can turn up anything."

"You think this is aimed at anyone in particular?"

"So far, no. So far, I'd guess it's a remarkably effective way to grab the whole U.S. where it hurts — for political purposes yet to be revealed. But we've got to check out everything. Another thing — keep everyone in and away from the press, will you? For now."

Martin nodded. The ambassador shot him one intense, private glance. "Martin — I'm fiercely sorry about this."

"Right. Get going, will you? I've got this fantasy of the sky going dark about six o'clock with the wings of F-16."

"Thanks for taking over here."

"Hell, I'm glad for something to *do*."

The American parents sat together in the lounge, in chairs drawn into a tight circle. It was determined that except for Steven's asthma, none of the children had serious medical or emotional conditions; and while the parents' own experiences were extensive and varied, there was nothing to make any of them seem like obvious targets for international terrorism. "Except that three of the kids — half of them — are children of a senator and a congresswoman. Don't forget that." Steven's intense, thin-faced father raised an index finger in warning.

"Right." The congresswoman's husky voice acknowledged the point. "The U.S. government looks like the main target to me."

Paula leaned into the group, her face taut with strain. "Elaine, you and Stan are Jewish, aren't you? What if these people *are* Arabs?"

Stan Goodman rubbed a hand back through his hair and scowled at the floor. "I'm not sure just being Jewish would mean trouble for Sidney. Arabs and Jews have lived peacefully together many places in the Middle East for centuries, and still do. But our summers in Israel have got me worried. It's Israelis and Zionists in general that lots of Arabs focus their animosity on."

"Does Sidney know enough to keep quiet about it?"

"I think so. But it's stamped right there in his passport."

"He's got his passport with him?"

"Yeah. We're big on independence and self-reliance in our family. He carries his own passport."

Paula sighed. "Well. Thank God for any independence and self-reliance in any of those kids."

The parents of the younger girl, Martha, had been sitting in silence. Now the mother spoke up. "I must say, I'm encouraged that they didn't hurt the children who were left behind; and they did make sure they were found promptly." Yes, they all agreed; that was reassuring.

Martin looked at his watch. Only half an hour had passed.

At three o'clock the ambassador returned with news. Before nightfall a plane would be airborne from Washington, bringing a top-level State Department team, several White

48

House representatives, and investigators specially trained for this kind of terrorist event. The President himself would be calling later in the evening. Meanwhile, he wanted to assure them that no effort would be spared in the attempt to find the children.

At three-thirty news from the hospital finally arrived. A new spokesman in the dark uniform of the military police began the official report, through an interpreter. The recovered children were all physically well, though experiencing considerable stress. All had given full statements. The guide, who still insisted on speaking to the American parents, would arrive soon. It was his belief that only two of the kidnapers were native Italians; these two had worn ski masks to avoid identification. The others he believed spoke Arabic. Because of this information the authorities were increasing surveillance at all major ports and along the northern land borders.

On the bus investigators had found cameras and tourist brochures, but no personal effects — except that between one seat cushion and the wall they had found Sidney Goodman's passport, which seemed to have been intentionally hidden there.

Elaine and Stan Goodman grabbed each other's hands as the other parents turned to them in a buzz of excitement. Yes, yes, the kids are using their heads. Martin saw Paula's shoulders slump slightly: muscles relaxing. For the first time he noticed the little hitch in his own shoulders, the steady pressure of muscles like a tourniquet around his lower ribs, the tautness in his face that kept his mouth from trembling. Muscles that had been tense for nearly twenty-four hours. In a moment of strange, objective sympathy for himself he put his face into the dark privacy of his open hand and rubbed the tired flesh.

In the hall, noise of an arrival. "Ernesto Vincenzo is here

49

now. You may question him, but the doctors say not too long."

The guide entered, leaning heavily on a policeman's arm. He was shorter and older than Martin had imagined, and the bruised face under the heavy white bandage was haggard. He stood, fists clenched tightly against his stomach, looking from one face to another. Then he opened his hands, began, "My dear friends" — and could say no more. With his hands still held out to them, he dropped his head and cried.

Six

Get up, boy! Come on, come on." Shaken awake,
Steven looked up at Assad. The dark face itself was familiar
enough, after what had seemed like days on the boat; what
was new was the Arab headcloth fastened around it.

"Fold up your blanket like the others. You will take it with
you." The engine had stopped.

Carrying his blanket, Steven climbed the stairs into darkness, under a sky bright with stars. Across a mile or two of
water lay the blackness of land, with not a single light visible. One by one the Americans were helped down the ladder and into a small open boat, where they huddled on rough
cross-seats or sat flat on the bottom. Assad and some of the
other guards — all now wearing the long Arab shirts and
headcloths — came with them. In a moment they were
moving smoothly toward shore. Jessica, sitting beside Steven, put her hand on his knee. He hoped she knew what the
dark land in front of them was, but he dared not whisper to
ask.

Not until they were very close could he see the black dock
reaching toward them — and then the truck, waiting at its
foot. An old pickup with a homemade, windowless top. He
wanted to point it out to Jessica. *Oh boy*, he would have said,

sounding bored — *here we go again.* He regretted bitterly that he couldn't say it aloud; it would have been so reassuring to hear himself.

He was led carefully past big holes in the rotting dock and hustled into the truck, having time to notice only the flat barrenness of the area. Way inland in the darkness he could see a high line of hills; but near at hand there was only flat, baked earth with very little growing. This was a spooky place.

Two guards followed them into the back of the pickup. Assad spoke softly before closing the tailgate. "If you are sensible, you will not be tied and gagged. So don't be foolish." There was a clanging of metal, and they were in darkness again.

It was going to be an awful ride. The truck was old and the road terribly rough. Leaning back against the side of the truck was murder. Steven and Jessica soon learned to sit back to back, with their blankets beneath them for cushioning.

The guards began to talk softly with each other, in the language that was so mysterious to Steven and yet, in its simple rhythms and full vowel sounds, with harsh little surprises, somehow appealing — as though it were a language his very bones had once understood. The relaxed mood of the guards impressed him. They felt safe now, he realized; wherever this was, they felt safer being here.

But the physical miseries of the trip grew worse. At first the road at least was flat. Eventually, though, it began to climb — a long, twisting climb that seemed to last forever. Day came; he could tell by a single pinstripe of light at one corner. The air inside grew hot. Finally the tilting of the truck lessened till they bounced along once more on level ground. By now he was breathless in the heat. His brain felt stunned, useless. He doubted that he could hold himself together much longer. Perhaps he would stop being. What could be beyond this long misery, except death? I want my mom, he thought. Dear God, please, I want my mother and father. For a while, very softly, he cried.

At last the truck stopped. Assad opened the tailgate, and they all covered their eyes against the fierce, flat light. "Everybody out. Here you are finally, at your vacation resort." They climbed stiffly out and stood squinting, staring in shock. Jessica took Steven's hand. On all sides there were only wild, rocky hills, almost completely bare. Here a tiny, squat tree with scraggled branches seemed to grow right out of the rock; there a clump of dusty gray weed pushed up from a patch of sandy gravel. But mostly there was gray rock — rock rising in small, sharp cliffs behind and to one side of them; rock falling off to a narrow ravine on a third side; rock sloping gradually off in front of them, then rising again.

Only when Steven looked again did he notice that there was, after all, a sign of human life — two little boxy huts, the same color as the rock. One stood directly in front of them; the other perched higher than the first, on an opposite slope.

Assad stood talking to a tall man in a gray headcloth. They were staring at the two girls and arguing. Finally Assad returned. "Get your blankets and jackets and go into that house."

The single room of the hut was empty, except for a very low, round table, which seemed to have been made from a packing crate, and a pile of rolled mats stacked against a wall. Three small square windows were cut through the thick mud walls. The two on the long side of the hut looked out toward the narrow ravine; the third, beside the door, faced front toward the other hut. Inside there was nothing to look at but the bare mud walls. In this ugly room set among dead rocks, it seemed to Steven that they must be a million miles from any place that was real.

Assad entered and leaned his hand against the wall. "So.

Here you are. This place will be your home till your country meets our demands."

"Where are we?" Gib asked.

"Ha!" Assad laughed. "I have told you the za'im has forbidden that you know such things. Why should you know? Americans have never wanted to know anything about the Arab world, even after you wanted our oil. So you shall stay ignorant."

The tall stranger entered, ducking his head at the door. He was carrying a rough-woven blanket in his hands, and he spoke sharply to Assad. Assad laughed again and shrugged. "This is Fuad. He is our host. All this land for miles belongs to him and his people. He will be good to you, because he is Bedu. Beduins are proud hosts. Now he is disturbed because he did not expect girls. Arabs do not believe women should be in public, looking for trouble. Now he will separate boys from girls."

Using a hammer and a long spike, Fuad fastened a corner of the blanket to a spot high on the wall. Then he turned to Jessica, frowning. "In Islam, man protect woman. Woman not married, be away from man. You American woman; you want talk, eat with man, I permit. But you sleep here, behind . . ." He looked to Assad for help.

"Curtain."

". . . behind curtain." He stretched the blanket across to the opposite wall and fastened it there, too, leaving the lower end loose for passage. The space they were standing in, small to begin with, was now smaller still.

Fuad picked up two reed mats from the pile against the wall and put them behind the curtain. "Woman sleep there. No man go there, or have very bad punishment. Man must . . ." He turned again to Assad, who finished for him: "He

54

says here among strangers you boys must be brothers to the girls, protect them like your sisters."

They all stood looking at each other awkwardly. Then Martha walked to the curtain, looked behind it, and turned back to Jessica with a shrug. "At least we get our own window." Watching her, Steven felt a wave of relief. It was the first thing he'd heard for many hours that sounded like home, like the voices of the teenaged girls next door — used to being bossed around by adults, bored by it even: shrug, sigh — "At least we get our own window." He held it tightly in his mind and hugged his blanket close.

The others seemed to relax a little, too. Jessica asked, "How do we eat?"

"Guards will cook your food and bring it." Assad made a wide sweep with his hand. "There are guard posts all around here. You are surrounded by armed men. No hamburgers and steaks, here! You will eat the way poor Arabs eat. It will be good for your souls."

"What about a toilet?" asked Sidney.

Again Fuad burst out in Arabic, his hands flying. Assad explained. "There is a latrine a little way down the ravine. No one can go there without a guard. Since there are girls here, Fuad will arrange a shelter around the entrance for more privacy." In fact, it seemed that Fuad was going to work on it at once. Assad followed, pulling the heavy wooden door shut behind him and dropping a bar into place with a clang.

It was the first time the hostages had been alone together. For a moment no one spoke. Sidney held up a hand in warning and went to look out the front window. Understanding, Gib and Jessica checked the other two. Then Jessica asked softly, "Does anybody have any idea where we are?"

A silent chorus of shaking heads. "It's someplace that bor-

55

ders on the Mediterranean," said Sidney. "How long were we on that yacht? Two nights and days?"

Gib nodded. "We could have gotten practically anywhere in that time."

Matt rubbed his forehead. "I'll bet this place isn't on any map in the world. I don't think that was even a road that we drove on to get here." They looked out the front window to where the truck waited, and beyond; there was nothing anywhere that looked like a road.

"So. We don't know where we are."

"I'll bet everybody's looking for us, though," said Martha. "Do you think they've found out about the green truck by now and that little dock place and everything?" She looked from face to face. Somehow everyone ended up looking at Gib.

He rubbed a hand through his hair. "Well, I sure hope so." He doesn't think so, thought Steven, and his stomach tightened.

Jessica sighed shakily. "At least by now all the experts in the U.S. are working on it. Maybe the whole world."

"You think it's on television and everything?" asked Steven.

Gib twisted a corner of his mouth. "You better believe it, Stefano baby. We may be the top story all around the world."

That was comforting. Steven looked out at the bleak rock again. Sidney's hand reached past him and took hold of a heavy bar set vertically into the window, "Hey, look! This thing's new. Somebody had time to get this place ready to hold prisoners. It's all dug in and set in concrete."

Gib went to look at the door. "This is brand new, too. Bet there never used to be a door here at all. A *heavy* baby. Hinges on the outside. Wouldn't do us any good to mess with that."

Martha returned from behind the curtain. "There's nothing in this place. Except the table and those mat things. And sand. I hear it grit every time I step."

"Nothing to use for lights, either," said Matt. "And water. What do we do for water?"

Sidney gestured toward the front. "There's a pail outside the door. A buck says that's it, and it has to be carried from a well somewhere."

Jessica turned to him. "How do you know all that?"

He looked at her oddly for a moment, then shrugged. "It's pretty obvious."

The sound of softly gritting sand made Steven realize that for some time he had been shifting weight from one foot to the other. His father never liked it when he did that. He felt a keen stab of homesickness, thinking of how his father would have frowned, puffing out his cheeks a little. "I've got to go to the bathroom pretty soon," he said.

"Okay, Stevie," said Jessica. "Let's see how this latrine system works." She went to the front window and called to two Arabs who seemed to have taken up guard duty. "Hello, out there. Somebody, please, we need some help."

Later, as the light in the room grew rosy and the heat began to lessen, Steven sat with the others around the low table, watching a slight, smiling, dark-skinned guard set their supper before them — a single bowl of grayish, doughy-looking lumps and a metal plate of what Jessica said were dates. There was also a blue enamel pot of tea. Above them, Assad leaned against the wall, grinning. "You pampered children don't know how to eat with bare hands, do you? Look, I have had spoons brought for you, and nice plastic cups for your tea. See what good care we take of you. Just like a Holiday Inn."

Steven looked at the sandaled feet beside him, higher at the belted shirt that fell to calf length, higher still at the white teeth and black eyes, wrapped about by the headcloth — the handsome face that wanted them to fear him and like him, at the same time. How could a man who looked so foreign speak of Holiday Inns? "We will bring your food, but you must clean your dishes afterwards."

Jessica looked up at him. "How can we do that?"

He laughed. "You are not a Bedu woman! Beduins wash with sand. But we have water for you, just like a Hilton. A whole bucket of water, every day. See, I will bring it inside. For drinking, for cleaning dishes, for washing your clothes, for washing before prayers. Only — you don't wash before prayers, do you? You turn to Allah with dirty hands. Or maybe you never pray anyway."

He straightened abruptly. "When your bowl is clean, call to the guards. They will take it away and allow you your last latrine trips. Then they will bar the door for the night. You have seen your sleeping mats, and you know where the girls must sleep. I warn you — Fuad will not tolerate any immorality. I will speak with you tomorrow." He left, and the grinning food-bearer followed.

"Is this all we get?" Martha leaned over the bowl. "What is this stuff? It looks like dumplings." She took a bite with her spoon and made a face. "Oh, gross."

Steven chewed his own bite slowly. It was a little like the lumpy hot cereal he'd eaten at his grandmother's once, but stickier and grittier and a little bit oily. Certainly it didn't taste good, and he wasn't hungry. He decided to make himself eat one whole dumpling thing and one date.

He had never eaten a date before. When he had bitten through the hard skin, it was surprisingly sweet; but then he suddenly imagined that it was really a big, tough-skinned bug whose insides he was tasting. He dropped it quickly and put a hand over his mouth so he wouldn't throw up. He glanced shyly at Jessica; had she noticed? Her head was bent forward so that her hair fell like two curtains beside her face, but still he could see — it shocked him — that her mouth was twisted, and tears brimmed at her lower lashes. Finally she put her hand over her face and sobbed.

Her crying seemed to wash away his own courage, everyone's courage. This is not real, Steven thought. God, please make this just a bad dream. He pressed the heels of his hands over his eyes and moaned softly.

For some time no one could speak. Finally Gib said, "Let's try the tea." He poured some and tasted it. "Not bad. Super sweet, but — not bad. Come on, Jessica, try this. Even if we don't eat much of that stuff, we'll get energy from this."

Jessica wiped her eyes on the short sleeves of her shirt and took the cup. They all sipped silently. Gib had helped them. Steven glanced at him gratefully.

When he looked back at the big bowl, a shiny black fly with iridescent wings was settling on it. As he watched, two or three others joined it.

"Yuck!" Martha waved at them. "Where did they come from?"

Matt, too, tried to wave them away from the food, but they promptly settled again. "Anybody want more?" he asked. "Come on, before they get worse."

Nobody did. "But we're supposed to wash the bowl," Steven remembered.

"It's probably not good to send food back," said Matt. "They might be insulted or something, and give us less next time."

Martha snorted. "That's fine with me."

"Come on, everyone, we've got to play it smart." Gib rubbed an eyebrow. "So how do we get rid of this stuff?"

They looked around the room. There was no place to hide anything. "Someone take it to the latrine and dump it? No —" Sidney answered his own question; "A guard always goes with us."

"Throw it out the window," said Jessica finally. "Toward the ravine, as far as we can. One dumpling at a time. Maybe animals will eat them in the night."

"It's a risk," said Matt. "But so is everything else."

"So, let's try it." Sidney went to the side window. "There's no one in sight. Who's a good thrower?"

"Gib is," said Matt. He carried the bowl to the window, and Gib tossed the unpleasant food out into the dusk.

Had anyone seen? They listened. Perhaps not. A glance of satisfaction passed among them. They had tried a trick together, Steven thought; they had been brave.

Next they spread out the reed mats. Matt groaned. "That's sure as heck not much to sleep on."

"We could sleep on our blankets," suggested Martha.

Sidney shook his head. "We're going to need them over the top of us. It's getting cooler already. Feel it?"

Steven did. It was a surprise, after the heat of the day.

"Well, we'll have to put something under our heads at least," said Jessica. "Steven, you've got your sweatshirt. Does everyone have something to use for a pillow?"

"Not me," said Sidney. "But I'll just use a corner of the blanket. I've slept on the floor before."

"So have I," said Martha. "But it was in a sleeping bag, on a yummy fat living room carpet. We watched *The Return of the Pink Panther*, and then we ate chocolate-chip cookies and cocoa —"

"Hold it," said Gib. "Cool it about food, will you?" He kicked his mat flat and sat down on it. "God, what I would

give for a shower. I'm sticky with crud a foot deep. The rest
of you look pretty lousy, too. Tomorrow morning we all can
wash."

"From one bucket of water?" Martha wrinkled her nose.
"The same one we drink from?"

"Ssst! Come look!" Sidney whispered from the front window. They crowded close and peered out toward the opposite slope, through air that was turning blue with dusk. There
Steven could see the guards gathering — barefoot, in their
softly belted long shirts and tucked-back headcloths — six,
then ten, finally nearly twenty of them. Some carried rifles
slung from their shoulders; and everyone carried a fat, tidy
roll of something tucked under his arm. "Prayer rugs," murmured Sidney. "Watch this."

The men set down their weapons, spread their rugs in two
straight rows, and then stood talking. The rugs — most of
them a rich dark red — lay waiting. "Those things are beautiful," explained Sidney. "Incredible tiny designs. All hand-
made."

Assad emerged from the other hut. Finally Fuad arrived,
laid his rug by itself in front of all the others, and called out.
Now the prayers began. "They all have to face the same way,"
Sidney whispered. "Toward their holy city."

"Mecca," added Jessica.

They moved together, with Fuad in front: sometimes
standing, sometimes kneeling on their rugs with their foreheads touching the ground, sometimes stretched out flat. At
certain points they spoke in unison; at other times they prayed
silently. Often they repeated a phrase that Steven came to
recognize: *Allahu akbar,*" which Sidney said meant, God is
great.

Finally they finished, rolled up their little rugs, and strolled

61

away. Two of them came back to the main guard post, where they squatted with their rifles beside them and lighted a kerosene lantern.

The hostages moved back from the window. "They're supposed to do that five times a day," said Sidney.

"Muslims are sort of superreligious, aren't they?" asked Gib. "Doing that right out in the open, and everything."

"Do you suppose their religion has anything to do with their kidnaping us?" Jessica looked from face to face.

"If it does, it's bad news," said Sidney glumly.

"Why?" asked Steven.

"Because it's religious fanatics — who are so sure they're right and everybody else is wrong — who make a lot of the trouble in the world."

Steven rubbed a shoulder against the wall. He wanted to say that he had felt better, seeing the Arabs praying in their strange way; it had made him feel they must be good people. Then he remembered that they had kidnaped six people and hurt an old man, so he must be wrong. Still, the memory of their prayers remained a secret comfort.

Later, a guard with a flashlight led him once more to the latrine. Hidden in a rough ridge of the ravine, it was approached under a section of black woven tenting, which had been stretched like a lean-to across the entryway. The guard handed Steven the flashlight before he entered and showed him where to shine it. What was he supposed to be looking for? Snakes? He glanced up at the strange dark face above him and started to ask. Then he stopped, still gazing into the stern eyes, suddenly overwhelmed by the great wall of wordlessness between them.

When the last hostage had been returned to the hut, the guard closed the door and lowered the heavy bar. Steven lay with his head on his folded sweatshirt and his blanket pulled over him. The mud floor beneath his mat was hard and unfriendly. Beside him lay Sidney, breathing quietly. Behind the curtain he could hear the girls moving about, trying to get comfortable. "You okay, Stevie?" Jessica called.

"Yes," he answered. Then — knowing he shouldn't ask — "How long do you guys think it will be before we go home?"

It was Gib who answered finally. "There's no way to say. We'll just take it one day at a time, okay?"

"And one *night* at a time," said Matt. "Has anybody found a way to get comfortable?"

"I'm too tired to care," said Martha, from beyond the curtain.

"You mean you've got built-in padding," said Sidney.

"I'm also too tired to get insulted."

They were quiet for a while. The guards had turned on a radio, and faint sounds of eerie music floated into the hut — a woman's voice in a wailing kind of song that shook itself through notes unlike any Steven had ever heard before. In the dark the sense of strangeness grew, swelling in his head like terror.

After a while Sidney spoke again. "Hey. Better not mention anything about my being Jewish. They probably know — but they may not. And Arabs aren't too big on Jews, you know."

"Sure." Gib's tone was reassuring.

"Sidney, are you a religious Jew?" That was Martha.

"Yeah, sort of."

"But not fanatic, of course." Jessica was teasing.

"My bar mitzvah's going to be September twelfth. That's the day I become a man. I've been studying with the rabbi . . " His voice suddenly dropped out from under his words.

63

Steven guessed the thought that had interrupted him: *if we're home by then.* Dear God, dear Jesus, let us be home by then. Let us be home soon.

In the dark, the bad fear had re-entered the room. Again Steven saw Ernesto's face being slammed down against the edge of the seat, saw daylight disappear as the doors of the truck swung in toward him. He sat up suddenly, trying to escape the terrible images. He rubbed his bare knees in anguish, and felt ridges in the skin that had been pressed there by the mat beneath him. Suddenly the ridges seemed a symbol for all that had been happening; this weird place and these bad-dream people were being pressed right into his skin, into his mind. It was like branding a steer. Would they own him, then? The thought terrified him. He must not let it happen; he must not let his bare legs touch the mat. He would sit up all night.

After the troubled silence, he started at the sound of Gib's voice. "Well, everybody try to get some sleep."

Jessica said, "Sidney, you'd better invite *us* to your bar mitzvah."

"Sure, it's a deal."

"In the meantime, let's hang in. Good night, Stevie."

"Good night."

There was a pause, and then suddenly — from Martha, he thought — a giggle. "Good night, John-Boy."

There was an answering snicker or two, and Steven realized that Martha had made some kind of little joke. Once again she had claimed this strange space for them as the people they really were, not as prisoners with the insides shaken out of them. The haunting Arab music still reached into their hut, but it no longer had authority there; the echoes of their own voices, of Martha's, now filled the space. *Martha* would not worry about pressing foreign creases into her chubby knees.

Now he wasn't so frightened. Still, it seemed best not to lie down again. So he sat with his blanket around him, till finally he slipped down onto the floor without even knowing.

Seven

Matt woke slowly, remembering at once where he was because of the hard floor beneath him, then dozing again to escape the grim details of reality. Finally he knew he was beyond sleep, rolled over slowly, and opened his eyes.

He was staring up through a bright shaft of morning sun at a minor massacre. The low ceiling was flecked with glistening black bodies of lethargic flies, which were disappearing one by one via the quick tongues of several small green lizards.

"At least we've got a *few* allies around here." Gib, too, was awake, lying on his back. "Go, lizards!"

"It's gruesome," said Matt. "Poor sucker flies don't stand a chance."

"I'm not sorry for 'em. They're too dumb to fly away. *I* plan to use my head." Gib sat up to look out the window. "Nothing happened overnight, I guess. Everything looks the same."

Matt sat up slowly; the load of numbed fear in his chest felt like a weight that would take special balancing.

"Hey, can I come out?" Jessica asked from behind the curtain.

"Sure," said Gib. "What did you think, we might be undressed? It's going to take paint thinner to get these things off me."

Jessica moved carefully past the sleepers. "Then you'd better find some this morning. We've got to get clean. I smelled us before I opened my eyes this morning. Any news?"

They shook their heads. "We can't expect things to happen *too* fast," said Matt. He rubbed a hand across the floor. "Hey, there's more sand now. There must be sand in the air, all the time. Do you think we're near the shore?"

Gib shrugged. "Or a desert, maybe."

Jessica waved a hand at the younger boys — Sidney neatly wrapped in his blanket with even his head covered, Steven slumped in an odd position. "I guess the younger you are, the better you can sleep on a hard floor. Martha's still asleep, too. She's something else. Here I am, sixteen years old and crying myself to sleep last night, and there *she* is — what, eleven? — acting like ho, hum, she's just been sent off to summer camp again."

"I don't know about Steven, though," said Matt. "I'm always afraid he's going to have an asthma attack."

Jessica blew out a long breath. "Well, he's been all right so far. Through four pretty horrible days. Maybe that's the worst of it. I mean—don't you think we could be released pretty soon?" Her tone was casual, but the fear in her eyes was stark.

Gib wasn't going to answer. "Well, yeah," said Matt. "I suppose it could happen anytime. Of course, we don't even know what they *want*, yet. But, sure, they could be negotiating right now. Dad would have all kinds of suggestions for strategies —"

Gib waved impatiently. "Dad wouldn't be allowed to have anything to do with it. With you and me involved? Forget it. Someday you'll have to learn your daddy isn't Superman."

Matt would never understand why Gib suddenly picked fights. Even in the middle of a kidnaping, in front of a strange girl. "Get lost, Gib."

Gib stood up stiffly and began to roll his mat. "Oh, I already did, Vereen." His tone was different now. "Haven't you noticed? We *all* did."

Breakfast was brought by the same friendly guard. He seemed to speak no English, but smiled broadly and slapped his chest to introduce himself: "Mustapha."

They looked at the pottery pitcher of milk and the bowl of pale, mashed beans. "Thank you, Mustapha," said Jessica.

"This is getting worse," muttered Martha. "That looks like it once might have been lima beans."

"We have to eat," said Gib. "Let's get on with it."

Matt dipped his spoon into the bowl. This time, it wasn't bad; the bland bean taste was improved by oil and garlic and a spice he didn't recognize. By steadily waving their free hands, they managed to keep the flies from settling in the bowl.

"The milk's a little weird," said Martha. "Where do they get milk way out here?"

"It's goat's milk, probably," said Sidney.

"Urg," said Steven, making a face. But later, Matt noticed, he drained his cup. In fact, they all did. Maybe hunger was helping them adjust; the bean bowl, too, was emptied.

They cleaned the dishes by pouring a tiny amount of water over them, rubbing them, and setting them back on the table to dry. Jessica spread her sweater over them to keep the flies off.

As they were finishing, Assad arrived with Fuad, carrying bundles of cloth. "Now we all sit down and have a talk."

Fuad, with a gesture, showed that he expected to be in charge of the meeting. "You no like *bazin*, yes? You throw."

"Last night," Assad explained. "You threw your supper out the window."

Jessica looked at Fuad. "Yes. We apologize. We couldn't eat; we were too upset. We didn't want to be discourteous by sending it back." Matt glanced at her in admiration.

Assad tossed his head. "That's stupid, to throw food away!"

Fuad silenced him with a raised hand. "All you are guest; I wish you to be comfortable. You like better the *ful mudammas?* This morning?" Several of them nodded.

"We give other food. You no like, you speak. You must eat like Beduin, but I wish you be comfortable." His frown seemed more like earnestness than sternness. It occurred to Matt suddenly that he could like this man, maybe even trust him — but, no, no, such feelings could betray him.

Assad put his hand on the pile of white and gray clothes beside him. "I will explain these things. Now you must all wear Arab clothing." He glared at Jessica and Martha. "*You* should not be here; so you must dress like boys. This *thobe*" — he held up a long shirt and a cloth tie for belting it — "and this *kaffiyeh.*" He shook out a gray headcloth and a braided headband. "You may wash and keep your own clothes, but you must wear these things."

"Speaking of washing," said Jessica, "if I may say so —"

"Speak," said Fuad.

"We could really use some more things. We need a pitcher or bottle so we can keep our drinking water separate. And some kind of soap, and towels, if possible. Paper for the latrine. Oh, and hair brushes or combs! And please, another pail of water." She spoke slowly, using pantomime to help him understand.

Fuad nodded. "You can have some. Pitcher, pail. But the guards . . . talk?" He got help from Assad, then went on. "The guards *complain* to get water. They must get own water.

But is not work for man. Where there is woman, woman must get water. So — you have more water. But you, woman, you must get. Guard walks with you, but you carry water for American prisoners." Jessica and Martha looked at each other, eyebrows raised.

Fuad's helpfulness encouraged Matt to try for more. "The flies bother us." He waved at the flies on the ceiling to show what he meant. "Is there anything we can do about them?"

To his surprise, Fuad began to grin. "Assad also. Assad not Bedu. You ask *Assad* give cloth for flies."

Assad gazed up at the ceiling with his eyebrows raised; was he embarrassed? Finally he looked at Matt. "Beduins are strong people. But you and I, we have lived in cities. We know it is better not to live always with flies. It is healthier. I have an extra mosquito netting. You can hang it over the table for eating."

What they did with it, later in the morning, was cut it into sections to fasten across the windows and the doorway. Matt, Gib, and Sidney attached them with crude supplies lent by Fuad, while the girls took the first turns at bathing at the back of the hut, behind a screen made of rusted sheet metal. Steven — in a long white thobe and kaffiyeh — stood guard for them, a small, straight Arab.

The girls took ages and used up all the water, so when at last they were finished — their faces shining and their wet hair as smooth as bare hands could make it — they set off for the well with an armed and grumbling Arab escort, each girl carrying a bucket. Covered by the desert clothing, they looked very much like Arab boys. Jessica's sandals fit right into the picture. But Assad had forbidden all other kinds of footwear, and Martha walked carefully as she tried out the rough terrain in bare feet.

They were gone a long time. Matt began to worry. "I hope

70

it was okay to let them take the girls off like that. Maybe we should refuse to let 'em ever split us up."

"A lot of good refusing would do." Gib was lying on his back, his eyes shut. "They can do pretty much what they like with us."

"No, Matt's right. We should refuse to cooperate with them." Sidney knocked the knuckles of his fists together. "They're terrorists. They won't respect people who aren't tough."

Matt shook his head. "I don't mean *that*. That would be asking for trouble. But I sure wish the girls would get back."

Eventually, they did. "My gosh," gasped Jessica, collapsing, her face sweaty again and now streaked with dust. "It must be two miles. Then you have to lower this piece of inner tube way down through a hole in the rocks to the water, and pull it back up. Over and over. And then carry the bucket back! Please, guys, use as little water as you can. This is murder."

Martha slid down the wall till she was sitting. "I may never move again. Look at my fingers. They're permanently curled."

"Did you see anybody?" asked Gib.

Jessica shook her head without opening her eyes. "Some goats. But no people, except for a few guards around a couple of black tents, in the distance."

"*Our* guards, you mean?"

"Yeah. The guy who was with us waved to them. Oh, I've never been so exhausted."

"At least you get out of this place," snapped Gib. "We've been nowhere except to the latrine."

"Believe me, I'd love to trade with you." Jessica pulled off her kaffiyeh and wiped her face with the hem of her thobe.

By the time the boys finished bathing, Mustapha had brought a woven basket piled with more of the flat rounds of bread they had had on the boat, and more strong tea in the blue enamel teakettle. From the window Matt could see the guards gathering on the opposite slope for midday prayers. When they lay prostrate, their clothing covered everything but their bare feet and the rifles beside them.

The afternoon grew hotter and hotter. No one mentioned washing the dirty jeans and shirts piled in a sorry heap in a corner. Sidney and Martha sat at the low table, inventing a game played with tiny pebbles, but Gib and Jessica leaned against the wall, looking the way Matt felt — exhausted with fear and waiting. Steven sat in a corner with his face hidden.

Finally Gib crawled to the front window and rested his chin despondently on a forearm. "There's not only nothing to do, there's nothing to look at, either, in this creepy place."

After a moment Jessica sat up and pointed to the long, windowless wall. "Think they'd be angry if we drew something to look at over there?"

"They might," said Matt. "This place must belong to someone."

"I won't do anything we couldn't smooth off pretty quickly if we had to." She went to the wall and laid a thoughtful hand against it.

"Want to know who it belongs to?" asked Sidney softly. "Some tribesman of Fuad's who gave up keeping flocks this year and moved to the city."

They all turned to stare at him. Gib asked the obvious question. "How do you know?"

"My family's been abroad a lot. We lived for a year in Rome, and I understand Italian."

"So what does that have to do with anything?" asked Matt.

"Well. I think most of the guards aren't from around here. They just speak Arabic to each other, as far as I can tell. But this is Fuad's home territory — his and his brother's, or cousin's. You know, that other guy who's tall like him, and wears the same kind of gray kaffiyeh? The guy who brought over the mosquito netting."

"Khaled," Jessica volunteered.

"Yeah. Fuad and Khaled. When those two talk to each other, they use some Italian words. When they want to talk privately, they speak mostly Italian. They were discussing the hut while I was tacking up mosquito netting." They gazed at him admiringly. "But don't let on I can understand Italian."

"Why not?" Steven's eyes were wide.

"Because when you're a prisoner, you keep everything you know a secret. Then maybe it can help you someday."

"What kind of place can this be, where the local Arabs can speak Italian?" Matt asked.

Sidney shook his head. "Don't ask me. I'm sure most Arabs don't."

Gib turned to look out the window. "Stevie, check that other window, will you? Any time we're going to really talk like this, we've got to be sure no one sneaks up on us."

"What I'd like to know is how Assad speaks English so well," observed Matt.

Using the handle of a spoon, Jessica had started to scratch a design on the smooth surface of the wall. "And with an American accent," she said. "And lots of references to American things. He must have lived there; I'd bet a lot on it. I think he's dying to tell us about it. He drops so many hints."

"He sure is a showoff," Gib observed. "Maybe it's on account of you, Jessica. He always stands like some guy in a catalogue, with his head thrown back and his eyes flashing. You've gotta admit he's a *handsome* dude."

Jessica shook her head. "He's showing off for all of us, and

73

I can't figure out why. Especially since he's so scornful of us."

"Anyway, we should get him to tell us about himself," said Gib. "We might learn something important."

Jessica's drawing was making Matt uneasy. "I sure hope nobody minds your doing that."

"Yeah. Me too," said Jessica. "But we need something to keep us company." As Matt watched, she completed the outline of a large, powerful-looking hand that angled sideways with an insistent pointing forefinger.

"Hey," he said. "Where have I seen that before?"

"It's God's hand. From the ceiling of the Sistine Chapel in Rome," she said. "We went to see it the day we arrived."

"So did we!" said Gib. "Michelangelo. Wow, that seems like centuries ago."

"What's he pointing at?" asked Steven.

"At Adam's hand. I'll do that next. He's just created Adam and now he's about to touch him and bring him to life."

"Hey, that's cool." Steven scooted sideways on the ground to get a better view. "Is there more than hands? Are you going to do the rest of the two guys?"

"I'm not so good with bodies. I'll just do the hands."

Martha sighed. "Isn't it time for supper yet? At home I'd be scarfing Oreos about now."

Mustapha brought supper — a thick black soup, more flat bread, fresh oranges. He gestured at the blue teapot with pride, until Jessica peeked into it to see what he meant. "Well!" she reported. "Peanuts in the tea. What a lovely surprise! Thank you, Mustapha." As it happened, they all agreed that peanuts-and-tea tasted good. And the soup was really okay.

Assad must have been waiting nearby. The minute their cleanup was finished he appeared in the door, obviously eager to talk. "Well! Mosquito netting on your windows, even a drawing on your wall. Dirty clothes in a pile. You have made your simple Bedu hut into a regular American pad."

If Assad was not going to be upset at the drawing, perhaps no one would be. Matt exhaled with relief.

Gib leaned forward with a quizzical smile. "Assad. How come you know so many American expressions?"

The Arab worked the muscles in his cheeks thoughtfully. It was self-conscious mannerism; Matt wondered whether he'd practiced it in front of a mirror. Finally he said, "Why shouldn't I tell you? Many things the za'im says you must not know. But this, I will tell you." He sat down on the floor. "I was personally chosen by the za'im to be in charge of you because I speak your language so well. And I speak it well because I was in the U.S. for three years as a student."

"Where?" Gib's expression was still casual.

"I was in a very prestigious program for engineering near where you — some of you — live. In Washington, D.C. I was your neighbor."

"Were you already our enemy then?" asked Sidney coldly. "Were you a spy?"

Matt's insides churned abruptly.

Assad stared at Sidney beneath a tightening frown. "I am no spy. I am the enemy of no one, except those who make themselves enemies of Allah and the order of his creation."

Gib tried to save it. "Maybe we've even been at the same place at the same time. Did you ever go to a Redskins game?"

Assad gazed at Jessica's drawing through half-closed eyes. When he answered he seemed to be addressing it. "I will say no more about my years in America. It was a very boring time. I am bored with thinking about it."

There was a strained pause. "I hope it was okay for me to

75

draw on the wall," said Jessica finally. "We thought it would be nice to have something to look at."

"It is of no importance that you draw on the wall." Then, after a moment, "What do those two hands mean?"

"They're from a painting in Rome. That one is God reaching out to touch Adam, to bring him to life."

"To a Muslim, that is blasphemous. We do not make images of Allah. But we are tolerant of the beliefs of others. While this is your house, we will permit your religious pictures."

There was another long pause.

"Do you — uh, know about Adam?" asked Jessica, making conversation.

"Of course! The story of Adam is in the Koran, as in your Bible. Except that the Koran shows Allah forgave Adam for his disobedience and honored him. Do you know why? Because Adam accepted for mankind the responsibility of knowledge. That is a good meaning. It is different from what your religions say. You — Christians and one Jew, yes? — you explain to me why you believe God did not forgive Adam."

They looked at each other, at a loss. He did not help them.

"I guess that's hard to answer without more time to think," Jessica said at last.

"Think! Why *think*? If you knew, you'd know, not have to imagine it." He turned to Gib. "Do you know why many Muslims have scorn for people in the West, for Americans? Say why!"

"I don't know. Because we are richer than other countries? Because we have so many cars and TVs and things?"

"Ha! You are all so ignorant. We have oil, remember? So now we, too, have TVs — even in homes where there are no water pipes, like this one. Radios! Even these guards have

76

radios, in every tent. Cars! In some Arab countries there are so many big American cars that people leave them beside the road instead of repairing them. It is disgusting. No. Why do we scorn you? You tell." He frowned at Matt.

It was risky to answer, risky not to answer. Matt chose. "Because we have so much power in the world, much more than most countries?"

"Bah!" He spat with disdain. "Your power is arrogance and rebellion against Allah. We do not envy that power. No. We scorn you because of the weakness of your religion. Do you say prayers?" There were a few hesitant nods.

"Ha! What is your prayer, a few silly words in your head? *Now*, because you are in trouble? That is nothing! For a Muslim, every day is built around prayer. Your holy Scriptures. What can you recite of them, so they will be your companion and light your way? Listen!" He threw back his head and broke into rhythmic Arabic that flowed like music. They listened in silence.

Finally he stopped. "Every real Muslim knows many parts of the Koran. But — you! What do you know?"

"I know the Lord's Prayer," said Steven softly.

"Ha! Good! And I know my own name!" But Assad's tone seemed less sharp when he spoke to the youngest one. "What else, the rest of you? Your Scriptures. Your psalms. How much can you say from memory?" There was a long silence.

He looked at Sidney. "You, a Jew. Do you even know what words are at the heart of your faith?"

Sidney's voice was low and vibrant with anger. "Of course. The Shema. I won't say it just to please you."

"Ha. You do not know it."

" 'Hear, O Israel: the Lord our God, the Lord is One.' "

"So. Then what does it mean?" Silence, while Sidney glared at him through narrowed eyes. "You do not know, do you?"

77

After a while Jessica spoke quietly. "I don't have much memorized. But my religion is strong enough to keep me from despising anyone just because they're different from me."

Then Sidney, his voice sounding like stones shaken in a fist: "My religion teaches me that every life is important and given by God. I would never be a terrorist and kidnap innocent people."

Assad suddenly pounded the floor. "Ah! Every innocent life is important, is holy! Yes? Your religion teaches you that? You? You?" He pointed to each in turn. They all nodded, sure of this one thing. "And all religious Americans think this?"

"Yes." Matt was ready to get into this. "At least, ninety-nine percent of them. Maybe there are some sick people —"

"Then why does your country make more and more new weapons that will kill millions of innocent people? *Millions!* And you say one life is important! Do you hear what you are saying?"

They stared at him. Finally Gib said quietly, "But we would never use those weapons. Unless somebody used them on us first."

"And then what good would they be to you, when it was already too late to save you?" He stared at Gib, forcing a response.

"Well, I suppose under some conditions we might be forced to use them first."

"So! You *might* use them first, after all. One minute ago you said never, now you say maybe! And what would force you to?"

After a painful silence, Matt said, "*I* don't think we'd ever use them first."

"Then why do you have them at all? No, the world is not so stupid that it can believe that. So the Russians race to make

78

weapons because you race, and everyone else in the world is put into greater danger every year, and you never give a single thought to all of *us*. Do not tell me each one life is important to you! You are lying! To me, or to yourselves!"

Assad's angry face was appalling. They should never have allowed this to happen. Matt's mind raced, searching for a way to calm him. Then he noticed Steven.

Steven had been sitting near Assad, frozen with fear. But now, incredibly, his mind seemed to be wandering. An edge of Assad's robe lay on the ground in front of him. With a shy hand, being careful not to touch it, Steven began to trace the outline of its curve along the floor. It was as though he very much admired the edge of white cloth. Now he gently smoothed the surface of the ground nearby, as though he'd really like to smooth the robe itself — straighten it, ease its wrinkles, stroke it gently. His small hand moved slowly, steadily.

Assad did not seem to notice. But he sat for a moment without speaking, and gradually his eyes began to lose their angry sheen. Finally he looked down at the boy. "You are tired of talk, yes? The others must have their lessons — but you are very young. It is time for you to sleep."

He stood up. "Tomorrow is Friday, the Muslim holy day. You did not know that, did you? Of course not. Fuad and I will drive many miles to a mosque for prayers. The guards will stay; Khaled and Mustapha will be in charge. You will give them no trouble." At the door he turned back. "Oh, here is something for you." He produced a white comb, which he handed to Jessica.

"It's mine!" she exclaimed. "Oh, great. Thank you."

They listened while he bolted the door behind him. "How could you *thank* him?" grumbled Martha softly. "After the way he was scolding us?"

79

"I thanked him for the comb, not for the brainwashing."

"Is that what it was? Brainwashing?"

"Nah," said Sidney. "That was just discussion. Arabs *love* political arguments. It's their favorite sport."

"I'd say it was a religious argument," said Jessica, cautiously trying the comb through a section of her long hair.

"There's not much difference, to an Arab."

Matt shivered. "It sure had Assad up the wall. Do you suppose the arms race is why we were kidnaped?"

"It's really strange," said Jessica. "I'm against nukes, but I didn't even get a chance to say so. The way Assad came on, there was no chance to discuss things rationally."

"He clobbered us," said Martha sulkily. "Don't talk about it anymore."

Later the oldest three sat together, waiting for their latrine trips. "What did you think of Steven's little number there?" asked Jessica softly.

"You mean, calming Assad down? It was terrific," said Matt.

"What are you talking about?" asked Gib.

"He just kind of patted the floor real gently until Assad shut up. It was amazing. I don't know if he knew what he was doing, but it sure did the job."

Afterward, Matt lay in the dark, waiting for sleep. Gib was within arm's reach on one side of him, Sidney on the other, but he felt enormously alone — alone, somehow, in the dark cave of his own head. Assad's furious outburst *had* been something like brainwashing, and it laid on Matt one more layer of misery.

Finally Gib's voice broke the lonely silence. "Hey, Sidney. How come you know so much about Arabs?"

There was a soft scuttle as Sidney checked the windows before speaking. "Stevie, you awake?" No answer. "Okay, I'll tell you older guys, but you gotta keep it quiet. My family lived a couple of summers in Israel, in a kibbutz. That's where I learned about Arabs. And living in the desert."

"Is this a desert?" That was Martha, from behind the curtain. "This is more rock than sand."

"Lots of deserts are mostly rock. And there's sand in the wind, here. I'd guess we're on the edge of a big sand desert."

"My gosh, you know Italian, and you've lived in Israel." Gib was impressed. "But you don't understand any Arabic?"

"Only a few words. But I'm quick with languages, and I'll pick up what I can. No kidding, though, lots of Arabs hate Israel and any Jew who supports it. So keep it quiet!"

"Hey," said Martha. "No wonder you know about goat's milk and stuff."

"Oh, I'm full of useful information. Here's another tip for tonight. Turn your shoes upside down before you go to sleep."

"How come?"

"So you don't wake up to find a scorpion hiding in one."

There was a muffled little scream and the soft plop of shoes being turned over.

Matt reached to turn over his own shoes — very quietly — just to be sure, and then lay back, thinking: that was funny, Martha jumping like that; that was really funny. Now he felt better. After all, there were some encouraging things in their situation. Apparently they were not going to be terrorized or seriously mistreated. Or really brainwashed. They had each other to talk to, and some new secrets to share, and sometimes humor. These things would help them do what they needed to — keep up their morale and hang on to their common sense. Until they were free.

"Everyone can use the comb," said Jessica, beyond the

curtain. "But you've got to be careful. Anyone who breaks a tooth can't touch it again. Period."

One day, one night at a time.

The next day felt different, beginning with the sound that woke them — the whining protest of the truck being started. Jessica groaned. "I dreamed that noise was someone coming to take us home. When are we ever going to hear what's really happening?"

With Assad and Fuad gone for the day, the guards seemed more casual. Several Matt hadn't seen before now came up from their tents, rifles slung over their shoulders, to investigate the huts and catch sight of the prisoners. In his cousin's absence, Khaled patrolled the area with an air of stern benevolence.

Mustapha, free of his supervisor's eye, lingered at every visit. He was fascinated by Jessica's drawing of the hands. "Fatima?" he asked, gesturing, when he came for the breakfast dishes.

"What?" asked Jessica.

He held his open right hand toward her, the fingers spread wide, then gestured again at the drawing. "Fatima?"

"No, it's not Fatima, whoever that is. This hand is Adam's, and this one is God's. Allah's."

Mustapha's eyes widened with surprise. But at lunchtime he brought a small metal charm to show them, a plump little hand, palm forward and fingers widely spread. "Fatima," he explained to Jessica, and launched an explanation in sign language.

"Well," she said afterward, "I guess the hand of Fatima means good luck, and Mustapha thinks *ours* do, too." She looked at her drawing. "I don't think 'luck' is what Michelangelo had in mind. But I'll take any I can get."

The girls went early for water. Each hostage was allotted two cupfuls of it for washing underwear, which was then spread on rocks behind the hut to dry. Gib was the last to do his wash. When the guard let him back into the hut, he gestured the others closer. "I just saw a plane. Flying that way, beyond the ravine. Not close; I could barely hear it. But it sure was a plane."

"What kind?" asked Sidney. "Could you tell?"

"No. A real little jet, like a Lear jet, maybe. Anyway, it's nice to know there are people *somewhere* around."

"We saw some other Arabs today, on the way to the well," said Jessica. "Way off. Two of 'em, moving a flock of goats. Our guard was that angry one, you know? With the real thin face. The one who walked us to the latrine last night. That guy gives me the creeps."

"Yeah, Umar," added Martha. "Is he just weird, or what? A couple of times today he said something real low and fast. I couldn't tell whether he was talking to himself or cursing at us."

"Anyway, when Umar saw the shepherds, he really tensed up; and he kept a watch on them the whole time. It made me realize the guards' job is to hide us from people, as well as to keep us from escaping."

Gib stretched. "They're afraid of the U.S. Marines, that's what. As indeed they'd better be. If negotiations don't work, just you wait, fellahs."

"There's an Arabic word just like that," said Sidney. "*Fellah*, just the way you said it. It means 'farmer.' "

"Gib. Don't joke about the Marines." Jessica was once again tugging at her hair with the comb.

Gib slumped back against the wall. "Who's joking? I spent the middle of last night hoping and praying we've finally learned how to make helicopters that can handle sand."

"Why sand?" objected Matt. "This is rock and more rock."

"But we think we're near a sandy desert; that's how we keep getting it on the floor and everywhere. Since we came here, the wind's been from — let's see, is that north?" He pointed toward the front door. "Yes, sure. Because the sun comes up over there, over the ravine. But anytime the wind changes, we can see whether we're getting more or less sand. Eventually we ought to be able to figure out which way the desert is."

Jessica leaned her head back and shut her eyes. "What good will that do? It's the *Marines* who would have to know where the desert is, so they could come rescue us. Even with a sandproof UFO or something, they'd still have to know where we are."

"Only if negotiations don't work," Matt added. "Washington ought to be able to settle this thing." But he wasn't really so sure, and he sighed suddenly in exasperation. "How are we ever going to find out *anything* about what's happening?"

The full heat of the day beat down on the little hut. Insects rasped loudly at the window netting. The resilient mood of the morning had dissipated; no one had anything to say.

Even suppertime and the gradual return of cooler air did not ease the sense of desolation. Again they watched the guards' prayers at dusk. Afterward, Mustapha and several others gathered at the main guard post, laughing and joking in a mood of Friday-night festivity. Their radio blared its peculiar music. Matt and Jessica watched from the window; there was nothing else to do.

After a while Mustapha saw them. He waved, then suddenly jumped to his feet and ran to Assad's hut. In a moment he was hurrying toward them, carrying a larger, impressive-looking radio. Inside the room, he sat on his heels and spun the knobs. When he had what he wanted, he grinned at them and bounded away again.

They stared at the glowing dial as incredible sound filled the room. The soft beat of the bass thumped against Matt's diaphragm; the twang of the steel-stringed guitar purred along the inside of his ribs. He looked at the others in astonishment as the familiar voice burst into bloom in the foreign air:

> *Well, if it rains, I don't care,*
> *Don't make no difference to me;*
> *Just take that streetcar*
> *That's goin' uptown . . .*

Jessica began to cry. "Oh, man," said Gib. "Oh, man." Sidney slapped Matt's shoulder, chortling with excitement. "Hey!" cried Steven. "That's *American* music! That's home!" Now the chorus, voices swinging into harmony:

> *Old black water, keep on rollin',*
> *Mississippi moon, won't you keep on shinin' on me?*

Martha was the first to jump to her feet. "Come on, you stupid turkeys. What are you sitting there for?" Her face lifted, her bare feet bouncing off the mud floor, she began to dance.

They all did. Offering their spines to the rhythm, shouldering the air, inviting the lovely home sound to flow down over every inch of their bodies, they danced in the gathering dark. With every step Matt could feel his battered heart and head draw comfort from the movements of his body. His very muscles now reassured him: I still have strength and memory. I am still myself.

Gib was howling with laughter. "It's incredible! Look at us, in our crazy Arab shirts. Did you see anything so ridiculous?"

"Dance the hell out of this place," said Jessica, through her tears. "Right now. Who knows how long this is going to last?"

It lasted for two more songs.

When it stopped, a brisk, British-sounding voice announced, "Good evening. It's nine o'clock and time for the news."

86

Eight

In an instant they had dropped to the ground around the radio. "Don't touch it," hissed Matt.

"In London, today, the Social Democratic party made a show of strength in the House of Commons . . ."

"Jesus," Gib swore softly. "Are they watching us?"

Matt peered out into the dark. The guards at the main post were deep in discussion, their own music blaring. "No."

"Stay there and warn us if anyone starts this way."

"Turn it down," said Jessica urgently. "They might hear it."

"Russian military activities along the Polish border are once again increasing . . ."

"I can't believe it's English!"

"Where is it coming from?"

"Shut up, shut up! Listen."

". . . expressions of concern over the maneuvers.

"After four days of silence, the United States government has in the last 48 hours received two major communications from 'Tawbah,' the Islamic organization claiming responsibility for the kidnaping of six American children in Rome. Yesterday's statement demanded that the United States ac-

cept responsibility for the current threat of a nuclear holo-caust and begin immediate, unilateral nuclear disarma-ment."

"Oh, no," Jessica whispered into her hand. "Oh, no."

"Today's communiqué declared that if the United States does not meet the group's demands, the children will be killed. It said, in part, 'This ultimatum dramatizes the fact that the U.S. response to our demands will indeed determine the fate of all its children, and of ours. If the U.S. continues in its present course, these six children will die soon at our hands, but no crime will be chargeable to us; we will rather be sparing them and their children the terrible death which, whether sooner or later, their parents' refusal to repent will have made in-evitable.'

"The United States has not yet made an official response to either statement."

The music began again. They sat frozen, staring at the ra-dio. Then Steven looked up at Gib. "Will the U.S. do what they said?"

"Of course not, Stevie. No way would we do that. Those demands are ridiculous."

The younger boy's chest began to heave. "But I don't want to die! Are they going to kill us?"

"I doubt it," said Sidney. "That would be dumb. Arabs al-ways threaten disasters, all over the place, without really meaning it." But his lips were shaking, and he put up a hand to cover them.

"Listen, everybody." Gib's voice was suddenly fierce. "You all look so freaked out, Mustapha will notice the minute he comes for the radio. We don't want him to figure out we heard the news. So *right now*, look normal or I'll clobber you my-self, you hear me?

"Number two. They're not going to kill us. Their demands

are crazy, but they won't get *anything* from the U.S. if they don't turn us over alive and well."

Matt's breath began to steady. "I think Gib's right. They *say* they're going to kill us, to get more leverage. But none of the hostages in Iran were killed, remember?"

Jessica lifted her head to look out the window. "Watch it, here comes Mustapha. Get ready to thank him for the radio."

"And look *happy*," growled Gib. "He just gave us this real nice treat, remember?"

When Mustapha had come and gone, they sat in the dark and talked. Their voices sounded too loud to Matt, and he understood: they were trying to fill the room with sound so the new terror would not have space to grow in. "Look," he said, his own voice loud, "now finally the U.S. has heard what these guys want, so there's a way to start talks. Now Dad and the others can get going."

But they couldn't keep up the conversation, and then the silence trembled. Matt stared toward the window, knowing that all their brave words couldn't soften the news they'd heard: what the kidnapers said they wanted was impossible, and what they threatened was death.

Eventually they heard the distant sounds of late-night prayers beginning. Suddenly Steven's voice broke their own silence. "I wish I could be out there with them, praying."

Sidney sniffed disapprovingly. After a moment Jessica said, "Well, we can pray where we are, can't we? In spite of what Assad says about us. Anybody remember the Twenty-third Psalm?"

Their voices took turns putting together what they could:

The Lord is my shepherd; I shall not want.
He maketh me to lie down in green pastures.

He leadeth me beside the still waters.
He restoreth my soul.
Yea, though I walk through the valley of the shadow of death,
I will fear no evil,
For Thou art with me.

"Not bad," said Gib, when they'd done the best they could with it. "We didn't have to be out there getting up on our feet and down on our faces all the time, either."

"*I* don't think that's so good," said Martha. "My grandmother would freak out if she knew I couldn't say the whole thing."

"We got the most important part," said Jessica. "Tomorrow maybe we'll remember the rest of it."

"Let me see that first one again." Martin Vereen reached across the ornate conference table in the ambassador's office. The State Department official slid the document toward him.

The ambassador waggled his fingers sympathetically. "Take your time, Martin."

Once again he read each word carefully, searching for clues.

> Tawbah, a pan-Islamic brotherhood, has taken hostage the children of American legislators to force the United States to face its responsibility for the nuclear disaster now threatening the world. In joint madness with the Soviet Union, the U.S. has driven the world to the brink of utter destruction. These two countries have taken the whole *world* hostage.
>
> Only if one of them will lead the way back, away from nuclear armament, will the world have a chance for a future. Both nations bear this responsibility, and soon Tawbah will take further action to hold the Soviet Union, as well, to account. However, we address the United

States first, because its guilt is greater. There are four reasons that this is true:

1. From the beginning, the United States has led the way in the development of nuclear weapons.
2. The United States remains the only country that has ever used nuclear weapons against fellow human beings.
3. Right now, nuclear weapons of the United States are so aimed that they could kill unimaginable numbers of innocent Muslims, of whom there are 50 million in the Soviet Union alone.
4. As People of the Book, it is the Christians and Jews of the United States — not the unbelievers of the Soviet government — who betray their faith. They share with Muslims the revelation that human beings have been ordained the caretakers of Allah's creation, within their proper limitations as His creatures. It is they who have turned from this truth and blasphemously crowned themselves terrorist controllers of the world, through their satanic nuclear inventions.

Therefore—Tawbah requires that the United States:

1. Acknowledge and repent its role in leading the world into the present disastrous course.
2. Immediately begin unilateral and verifiable disarmament of all nuclear weapons . . .

He sat staring at the paper for some time before finally letting it fall softly to the table.

"Want to see the new one again, Senator?"

"Death threats. No, good Lord, I've seen enough of that." He looked around at the waiting faces. "You're sure both communications are bona fide?"

The man from State drew from a thick manila envelope two small items, which he laid in front of the senator. "Jessica

Portere's learner's permit came with the first statement. Your boy's library card came with the latest one."

The dog-eared bit of white cardboard with Matt's name on it triggered a memory of ordinary family life that hit him like a shock wave. He struggled past it. "Okay. But who the hell are these people? How do we know they're really Muslims? Who's ever heard of demands like these? And the language! Whoever wrote these statements is either extremely competent in English, or has one hell of a translator."

"We've got a group of Islamic experts convening back in Washington, as well as Professor Rauf's group here." A dark-skinned, scholarly-looking man at the end of the table courteously inclined his immaculate turban. "And of course the CIA and Interpol connections. Even the PLO's intelligence organization is cooperating with us. So we ought to find the trail soon. But so far — do you want to report, Majid?"

The Arab leaned forward and spoke in heavily accented English. "We believe the group is indeed Islamic. The argument about man's stepping beyond his creaturely limitations is sound Koranic doctrine. Of course, we must be very clear, Senator — the group is not part of any recognized Islamic body, and such bodies are now publicly condemning this terrible deed."

"You've found no one who has heard of the group before this?"

"No. But several Islamic universities — all of which are most eager to help, Senator, and deplore this act — do report some recent student interest in the theological implications of the arms race. For example, in both Karachi and Cairo —"

"But these do not sound like Middle Eastern documents! Excuse me, Professor. If they are Islamic products, why do they sound as though they were written by Westerners?"

The heavy eyebrows rose slightly. "I have a theory. I suspect that this movement consists largely of Middle Eastern Muslim students who have studied in the West, especially the United States — people who are torn between two cultures. There are thousands of such young Muslims, Senator. Did you know that? Each year their governments send them out — to the U.S., England, France — praying that they will learn modern technological skills, without losing their Islamic identity. I think you may have little understanding of the torment that cross-cultural experience can mean for a young Muslim."

"But that explains nothing of how this group became so dangerous," said Martin.

"Dangerous." The tips of the professor's fingers brushed the papers in front of him. "What group of human beings is not, especially when they are frightened? And do you doubt that this outlaw group finds *you* and your colleagues in Washington, always calling for more nuclear weapons, very 'dangerous'?"

They gazed at each other. "No," said Martin finally. "I can understand that. Tell me why you think these terrorists have been students in the U.S., and somewhat seduced by the experience. Because the written English is so natural?"

"Only secondarily. Consider — who do they think may save the world, if anyone can?"

"Themselves! By kidnaping children!"

"No. The United States of America, Senator! Do you not see? They give four fine reasons for demanding that you, before Russia, lead the way back from the brink of disaster. (And they *are* fine reasons, are they not? Forgive me, but I do admire them.) But those are the public reasons, not the secret one. They chose to pressure the United States first because they believe that at heart you do wish to value all human life. They even believe — simple, naive students — that they can make you respond to them, make you hear a call to conscience! Senator, to me this swaggering document reeks of a wistful longing for America to become a moral giant and lead the world to safety. Frankly, I am both embarrassed and moved by its naiveté."

For the moment, Martin could only stare.

The man from State cleared his throat. "Of course, gentlemen, there's another possible motivation for these demands, quite apart from any U.S. response."

The ambassador turned toward him. "Which is?"

"World opinion."

The ambassador slammed a fist onto the arm of his chair. "You can't be serious. You think they could believe that kidnaping children would rally world opinion in their favor?"

"I think it's quite possible."

"That's absurd. Read the newspapers, man! Editorials in dozens of languages have been scorching the paper they're printed on."

"That was before the first statement was received, Mr. Ambassador. Beginning yesterday, we've been getting very different reports, even from usually friendly papers like the *London Times, Frankfurter Allgemeine, Asahi Shimbun.* They begin the same way — this is an inhuman act against innocent children, and so forth. But they end up saying, 'Yet in the long run, "Tawbah" may be right; the lives of these six children, however precious, surely would pale before the increasingly possible destruction of millions.' "

The ambassador grimaced. "Sweet Jesus! Our allies, too?"

No one answered.

Martin was suddenly impatient. "Well, I'm grateful to all

94

of you. You'll issue a press release, Tom? I'll report this meeting to the other parents as soon as I get home."

The man from State began to pile his papers. "You're flying back tonight, Senator?"

"Yes. Now that we're sure the children are out of Italy, I'll feel closer to developments if I'm in Washington."

They all stood. Their wordless sympathy suddenly swamped him, and he couldn't speak. Professor Rauf extended his hand. "We will all do everything we can, Senator."

Beside him, Paula sat with her eyes shut. If he could have borne the darkness, he would have done that, too; this flight was so obscenely reminiscent of the last one. They had sat just like this, he and she, with their sons behind them. Impossibly, that had been little more than a week ago.

Somehow he could not shut his eyes; he could not even sit still, as she could. He had thought the flight home would bring him relief, because it meant he was returning to the center of political power on which he now was personally relying as never before. Instead, it was feeling like stark betrayal. Physically, he had turned his back on his boys.

He looked around the cabin for things that would distract him, but he could see nothing that seemed real — nothing but his own hands, twisting in his lap, and Paula's face. She looked exhausted and much older; with her head back like that, he could see a new hollow under her cheekbone.

As though she could feel his gaze, she opened her eyes and looked at him.

"You wanted us to stay there, didn't you?" he said. "Till the kids are back."

"I still think there are more clues there, to be discovered.

95

There *must* be. It's incredible that they haven't found more."

"We weren't helping find them, just by staying. And from now on, all the news will go right to Washington, first."

She shut her eyes again. After a while, he said, "Are you angry at me for insisting we go home? All the other parents have left."

"*You* have lots to go back to. The White House is waiting to talk to you about making some big statement. *I* go home to ticking clocks in an empty house. And the boys' laundry in the dryer, waiting to be folded!"

He winced. "Ah. Damn."

Still, after a moment she reached for his hand; the pressure of her fingers reassured him. Finally he could rest his head back. But as his breath steadied, his heart seemed to beat with increasing violence. He had to be careful not to squeeze her hand too hard. Emerging from beneath all the rest of it was rage.

It was suddenly suffocating. He released her hand and sat forward, feeling his face flush and the pulses in his neck pound. Rage. He must get this under control. "I'll be back."

Mercifully, no one was using the tiny lavatory. He locked the door and slapped his hands over his mouth to hold back the sound. *You bastards. If you hurt any of those kids I'll kill you with my bare hands. If you touch my boys so help me I'll tear your throats open . . .*

When at last he opened his eyes, the face in the mirror was contorted and livid. And — the discovery surprised him — it was bleeding briskly. From three deep, crescent-shaped slices made by his own fingernails. He reached for a paper towel.

Nine

The morning after the news broadcast, the weather changed. Matt woke already hot under his blanket, and there was sand everywhere. "The wind's changed," announced Sidney, back from his trip to the latrine. "It's coming from the south now." He pointed toward the girls' end of the room. "That must be where the desert is."

"It's funny," said Steven. "I can't see sand in the air, but it gets onto me. Does it get in your beard, Gib?"

Gib put his hand to his chin, as though the word surprised him. He *did* have a beard starting. "Yeah, it does."

Matt rubbed his own chin. Only a few scraggly hairs to show for the endless time that had passed. "What day is this?" he asked.

"August fifteenth," answered Jessica. "Only six days since Rome. It seems longer than the whole rest of my life."

"I guess we'd better make a calendar," said Matt, feeling grim. "We could scratch it on the wall."

"Let me be the marker. Please?" Steven got up on his knees. "I used to do that at school. I'll mark today, and tomorrow I'll mark tomorrow. And maybe after that we'll go home." Jessica made the calendar, and Steven marked Saturday, August 15.

Today it was not the sullen Umar who escorted the girls to the well, but someone new. "His name is Sadik," Jessica reported afterward. "What a relief! He's not frightening at all. You saw how young he is — just about our age, I'd say. I think he'd like to be friendly, but he doesn't dare. So he's superpolite."

"What're you talking about?" Martha screwed up her face. "He scarcely even looked at us!"

"That's what I *mean*," said Jessica. "He acts as though it would be rude to look. Besides, he kicked some sharp stones out of your way, Martha. Because you were barefoot."

"Big deal." Martha touched the new blisters on her hands exploratively. "I'd a lot rather he'd just carry a pail."

The day dragged brutally. Matt grew tired of waiting at the windows for some kind of news; tired of watching the others do the same. There was one good thing: Assad and Fuad had brought back fresh food from town. The hostages ate oranges at the midday meal. At supper there were fresh tomatoes and, for the first time, meat — chunks of lamb, cooked with cereal and vegetables into a stew.

"Oh, Mustapha, yum!" exclaimed Martha. "Even with sand in it. More like that, please!"

But there was no more like that. By the next day they were back to the familiar beans, flat bread, dates. "The vitamin content of this diet must be atrocious," said Gib, glowering.

Sand was still in the air, sticking in the sweaty creases of Matt's skin, sometimes even gritting between his teeth. Relief from it, as from boredom, came only with meals, brief trips to the latrine, the welcome oblivion of sleep.

But *waiting* for sleep, alone with private fears, was the hardest thing. Even getting ready for sleep became a test of courage. Matt soon discovered that everyone shared his dislike of the evening latrine trip. "In the dark, that's a real scary place," said Steven. "There could be snakes in those rocks."

"It's Umar that scares me," Jessica countered. "I wish he wasn't on duty so often in the evenings. I think that guy really hates us. I wonder why. All those dirty looks!"

"He carries a knife tucked into his belt," said Matt. "Anybody notice? Once he muttered something at me and grabbed hold of his knife. That's pretty hard to ignore."

"I don't ignore it," said Sidney. "When he curses at me, I curse right back."

"What?" Gib's head snapped up. "Sidney, what do you think you're doing?"

"He's trying to scare us! The more he thinks it works, the more he'll do it."

Matt shook his head. "Sid, you don't know that. What if he's just looking for an excuse to make trouble?"

Scowling, Sidney slouched lower against the wall and folded his arms. "I don't care what you guys say. People gotta keep their spirits up. You gotta resist. Can't you understand that?"

They argued. One morning Sidney spotted Steven marking the calendar after breakfast, instead of before. "Steven! You already marked today!"

"No, I didn't."

"Yes, you did! This is Tuesday still, not Wednesday."

"I forgot to mark it this morning."

Sidney sputtered. "No, you jerk! I saw you mark it!"

Matt was irritated. "Cool it, Sidney. He's just a kid."

"Shut up, Matt." Gib glared at him. "Who invited you into it? Steven can take care of himself."

"So? Who invited *you* into it, either?"

"*Somebody's* got to tell you when you're acting like an ass."

Sudden anger brought Matt up to his knees. But now Sidney was frantic, commanding everyone's attention. "We've *got* to know what day it is! Don't you see? We have to know when Friday is!"

Jessica shushed them with a gesture, then checked the windows. The argument had evaporated. "That's what we're all waiting for, isn't it?" she said. "Friday. And maybe another chance at the radio. Look, Sidney. We'll know it's Friday when Assad goes to town. And if he doesn't go, it doesn't matter what day it is. We'll never get the radio when he's here."

Gib wrapped his arms around his knees. "Listen, you guys. That was pure luck. It may not happen again. If Mustapha stops to think, he may realize Assad would be mad as hell. Besides, what we might hear on the radio isn't that important anyway. What's important is that we get free, and *that's* not going to be on any news broadcast till it's happened."

Matt was tired of Gib's pronouncements. "We can't help wanting to hear what the U.S. says in response."

Gib snorted. "There won't be any response. You don't seriously think we'll agree to any of those insane demands?"

"Of course not! But Dad says first you get the conversation going and then start building trust —"

"Trust? With terrorist kidnapers? Forget it. We'd be crazy to make any response."

"We'd be crazy *not* to. Dad will think of something —"

"Oh, for God's sake, Matt. Your father doesn't make U.S. foreign policy."

Again something made Matt's anger cool abruptly. "He's your father, too, Gib." Gib turned away and went to the window.

"Listen, Sidney, I keep this calendar *right*." Steven's voice was sonorous with hurt pride.

100

"Oh, Lord," groaned Jessica. "I wish to heaven it was time to go for water. You guys are driving me crazy."

That afternoon there were strangers nearby. The sound of a truck approaching — a shock in itself — was followed by shouted greetings. Matt's heart jumped, and he scrambled to the window with the others. In a minute the young Sadik hurried into the hut, gestured politely for the Americans to sit down, and stationed himself at the front window. Matt's first wild hopes sagged; Sadik was too calm for this event to mean anything really exciting. "Nothing to do with us," Gib whispered, screwing up his face with disappointment.

For a couple of hours they sat, bored, hearing only an occasional distant shouting match in Arabic. For much of the time Sadik stayed resolutely on the job, his gaze riveted out the window. Matt could sense his curiosity, however, and eventually he began to allow himself fleeting glimpses of the interior of the hut. Once, in spite of his obvious efforts, his glance directly crossed Matt's — and he flushed with surprise and confusion. Matt couldn't help grinning back. Finally the truck engine sprang to life and Sadik let them move again, nodding solemn regret for their discomfort as he left.

The next day there was more of the same. This time they spent the whole afternoon sitting on the floor under Sadik's guard, and the comings and goings seemed endless. Eventually there was a startling new sound: loud metallic scrapings and clatterings.

"Tools," said Matt later, when they were again free to talk. "Long-handled tools being dragged out of a truck."

"Maybe it's more guns!" said Martha, her eyes wide.

Gib shook his head. "You don't treat guns like that. Besides, they'd sound different. I wonder what's going on."

At suppertime a strangely glowering Mustapha brought rice balls, thumping the big bowl down on the table noisily. Gib raised his eyebrows in inquiry. Mustapha rolled his eyes to heaven, pointed accusingly out the window, and acted out an angry conversation in which he took several parts, before stomping away. Clearly, whatever was happening was something he didn't like; but the hostages were as mystified as ever.

Fortunately, when Assad dropped by a little later, he was in a chatty rather than an argumentative mood, and after a few minutes Jessica approached the subject. "Tonight at supper Mustapha seemed — thoughtful. Is he okay?"

Assad grinned. "Mustapha is angry. All the guards are angry. Now they must do some real work." He looked around at them, enjoying the storyteller's power. "Shall I tell you? Yes, I shall. This place, all around, belongs to Fuad's tribe. This summer Fuad is permitted to use these huts — for special purposes. But now his sheik sends a message that Fuad must have work done on the land so that next spring food will grow better. So now I command that the guards must take turns doing the work. Oh, they are so angry!" He laughed with delight.

"But how can anything grow here?" Matt was amazed. "This is all rock, with a little sand blowing around on top."

Now Assad could play teacher. "Behind here, way back, are some places with a little soil, where a grain can grow — I think it is what you call barley — *if* there is rain in the rainy season. This kind of place is called a wadi. It is a very shallow path along the ground, where the water runs if it rains. The problem is, the water runs through too fast and then is gone. More barley could grow in the wadi if the water could be a little trapped. So now, before the next rainy season, the Beduins must build little walls of stones across the wadi, to slow the water. What is the English word for the water walls in the Netherlands?"

"Oh," cried Steven. "The dikes!" Then he looked around and blushed proudly.

"Yes," said Assad. "That is the word." Again his teeth flashed in laughter. "So these guards, who are *not* Fuad's tribesmen, must help build dikes across the wadis, and they grumble like mad. That is very funny." Then, abruptly, his face darkened. "Americans who spend so many minds, so much money studying how to kill more and more millions of people in one hour should know about this — about places where people still struggle to make life better. Moving one heavy stone at a time. Is this even the same world you live in?"

Jessica leaned toward him, a hand held out timidly. "Assad. We have been waiting to tell you, we're against nuclear weapons, too. Some of us have worked for a nuclear freeze."

His frown didn't change, but Matt noticed a slight pause before he answered. "A freeze is nothing. Almost nothing. All the present weapons would still be there, all the danger to the world, all the blasphemy to Allah. If you *really* cared, you would work every day, all day — as Tawbah does — to show the world that it must change. If you cared, you would have passion, and it would guide your life."

He left them all in a sour mood. "I'm getting sick of this," grumped Martha. "It's bad enough to be kidnaped. Now we have to sit in the middle of nowhere and be lectured about nukes! When we don't even have running water! It's so —"

"Incongruous," volunteered Matt.

103

"I mean, look. I'm eleven years old. I go to school. I take drum lessons. I have a zebra collection. I'm a *kid!* What do I have to do with nukes? It's so ridiculous."

"We should have passion, he says," muttered Gib. "I'm working up a passion, all right. Oh, man, how I'd love to pulverize Assad."

"*Real* zebras?" asked Steven after a moment, hesitantly.

"Sure, Stevie," Martha answered, glowering. "Real zebras. I keep them in the laundry room."

He absorbed this. Then he shot her a quick, reproving glance. "They *could* be real. You could be rich. How do I know?"

"Teachers' families are *never* rich. Don't you know *anything?*"

That night Umar again came to take them to the latrine. This time, instead of taking them in any order as before, he stood at the door and with rough gestures indicated that Steven should go first.

Surprised, Steven obediently got to his feet and followed him.

"Oh, that guy," murmured Jessica, hugging herself and shivering. "Now he's going to play games with us."

"I don't like this," said Matt. On impulse, he went to the window facing the ravine and knelt there. By pressing his cheek against the side edge of the window opening and peering as far forward as possible, he could barely see bouncing beams from Umar's flashlight as the man and boy followed the path to the latrine.

Out — and back. Then, as Steven sat down again, Umar gestured to Martha. Matt stayed at the window to watch. Out — and back — the bobbing light again being all Matt

104

could see of their progress. The next turn was his own. Except for the heavier pounding of his heart, the trip was uneventful; Umar was silent, and Matt, too, said nothing.

Next Jessica, then Gib. Finally Umar stood staring at Sidney for several seconds before gesturing at him.

"Can you really see them, Matt?" asked Jessica, when the sound of their departing footsteps had faded.

"In a minute I'll be able to. There." The light moved into his range of vision, bobbed steadily away from him, and disappeared. In a few minutes it reemerged. Matt sighed with relief. "Good. Here they come back."

But suddenly the beam flashed wildly upward, sideways — and disappeared. Matt heard a series of thuds and a faint cry. Sidney's voice.

He grabbed the bar in front of him and began to shout. "Sidney! Umar! What is it? What's happening? Sidney! Help, someone!"

Gib and Jessica were behind him at once, pressing against him, trying to see, too. "What is it?" cried Jessica.

"I heard someone hitting the ground, and then Sidney hollered." Matt raised his voice again. "Help! Sidney! What's happened out there?"

Suddenly they could see the flashlight again. Then it angled sharply away — and met the beam of a second flashlight, approaching it from the direction of the other hut. The two lights met, and both shone for a moment straight into the face of Sidney, who stood with an arm across his eyes.

After a little while, the lights began their separate return trips. Umar's bobbed back toward them. Matt felt Jessica shudder with relief as she moved away. Against his cheek the window edge was slick with sweat.

Sidney stalked back into the room defiantly; but when Umar was out of earshot he dropped to the floor, shaking, as they clustered around him. "Oh, man. I thought I'd never see you again."

"What happened?"

"What did he do to you?"

"I fell down. Umar won't shine the flashlight where I walk anymore; he makes me stumble along in the dark. Anyway, I tripped on a rock and the next thing I knew, he had his knee on my chest and his knife against my throat. Hey, did it cut me?"

They bumped heads together, trying to see. "No," said Gib, "but if you were shaking then the way you are now, it would have."

"He *held* it there and growled something at me. I really think he wanted to kill me. Am I ever lucky Assad came out!"

Jessica was still shivering. "I think Umar really hates Americans, and maybe he hates Sidney especially."

"Because Sidney's Jewish?" asked Martha.

"Maybe. Or because Sidney curses back at him. That man really terrifies me."

Matt blew out a long breath. "You've got to stop provoking him, Sidney. Look, all we have to do is stay cool so Dad and everyone else can get on with getting us home. Okay?"

Now Steven crawled close. "That guy is scary, Sidney. Please don't make him angry anymore."

Sidney rested his face against his knees, which still shook. "I'll think about it."

Later, when Matt thought he was the only one still awake, Gib spoke softly. "I'm tired as hell of all your crap about Dad getting us out of here. Do you honestly believe that?"

Matt couldn't see his brother's face. "Of course I do. Dad's turning out to be one of the best negotiators in Washington. When the heck are you going to see that?"

106

"When the heck are *you* going to see how fake you are, playing up to him the way you do? Coming on like superkid so you can get all those stupid strokes from him and everybody else. Geez, it pisses me."

Surprised at the intensity of Gib's anger, Matt lay in confusion for a moment. Finally he turned on an elbow. "Gib — where the hell are you coming from? What's the matter?"

"I'm just tired of your showing off, that's all. You had to make such a big deal about Sidney's falling down out there. Shouting like that. Acting as though his life was in danger and your making all that noise was going to save him. You scared Jessica to death."

This was off the wall. "Wait a minute. *I* didn't scare Jessica, Umar did. And Sidney *was* in danger out there. Are you telling me he wasn't?"

A pause. "I'm just saying I'm sick of your showing off."

Matt blinked hard into the dark. "Let me get this clear. We're arguing about me and Dad. Right?"

"You got it."

"And that's all?"

"Right."

"Fine. Then "can" it till we're home."

He rewrapped his blanket and stretched out again with his back to his brother. He had lipped off at Gib much more than usual, and probably deserved a return blast; but even though his heart was pounding in anticipation, his head knew Gib wouldn't respond. Gib, too, would have sensed, as he himself just had, that they were on dangerous ground and it was time to shut up. Because it *wasn't* just their father, a million miles away, that they were arguing about.

Lying on his side this way, he was even more aware of the place on his back that he had been conscious of ever since

Sidney's return. A warm, wonderfully sensitized place. The place where Jessica, rushing with Gib to join him at the window, had pressed against him.

Friday at last. Assad and Fuad left early in the truck. Perhaps because it was the holy day, work at the wadi was suspended. Yesterday they had listened to the sounds of the work crews being organized, leaving, returning; but now there was nothing to hear, nothing to watch from the window except an occasional lizard scuttling across the rock, an occasional sparrow — and, of course, the prayers of the guards, marking noon and midafternoon. Nobody wanted to do any of the things that had been diverting enough before — planning imaginary homecoming banquets, taking turns describing the teachers they hated most.

They complained. "I'd give *anything* to open my eyes and see something different," moaned Martha.

Gib said, "Jessica, rub those hands off the wall and draw something else up there. I'm getting sick of 'em." By now all kinds of sketches and games had been scratched into the mud, but Jessica's big drawing on the long wall still dominated.

"Oh, no." Steven's tone was anxious. "I like them there."

"Well, then make 'em *touch* or something," said Matt. "Looks as though poor old God keeps reaching and reaching and never quite makes it. It gets to you."

"I'll think about it," said Jessica.

Delayed excitement frayed their nerves. "Sit *still*, Matt, will you?" growled Gib. "You're driving me bananas."

"I *am* sitting still. As still as you can on a dirt floor, leaning against a mud wall, for gosh sakes."

"You're *breathing* weird. You hold your breath a long time and then give this great big sigh. You're expecting too much. We probably won't even get to use the radio. Or it'll be the wrong time. Even if we do hear the news, it won't tell us much."

"It might give us a hint of what's really going on."

Gib rolled away. "Look. Just shut up and breathe normally, will you?"

No one was hungry for supper. Mustapha looked surprised at how much food was left in the bowl. At last it was time for the sunset prayers, and afterward—to their great relief—festivities at the guard post began.

Matt crowded with the others at the front window. "Come on, come on, Mustapha," he urged. "Remember us."

"Somebody wave and get his attention."

"No. We shouldn't look as though we care so much."

At last Mustapha looked their way, waved, and went to Assad's hut for the larger radio. They moaned with relief.

In a few minutes they were again alone with their own music. This time they were in no mood to dance. The familiar songs, which a week ago had seemed so short, now seemed to last forever.

"What if we've missed the news?"

"No, no, I don't think so. Just wait."

Finally, the same British announcer — and after several unrelated, excruciatingly long news items:

The United States government reports no new leads in the kidnaping of six American children. The White House continues to offer no official response to the demands of 'Tawbah,' the Islamic group claiming responsibility. Usually reliable sources in Washington report that the White House considers the demands 'outrageous' and 'unworthy of reply.' Senator Martin Vereen, the father of two of the kidnaped children and a member of the Senate Foreign Relations Committee, yesterday told reporters he did not believe the government should negotiate with terrorists.

109

"Today in Kabul, Afghan forces claimed victory —"

"Look out!" whispered Jessica. "Mustapha!"

"Be cool, everyone." Gib quickly flopped down on the floor with his arms behind his head. Matt leaned back against the wall and tried to look bored.

Mustapha burst into the darkening room, his eyes wide with alarm. He snatched up the radio and snapped off the sound.

"Aw, please," said Jessica, "we're waiting for some more music!" She strummed an imaginary guitar as translation.

Matt picked up her cue and made a soundless flourish of drums. "Yes, please, Mustapha — music!"

The answer was unmistakably negative. Mustapha was sorry, but — no, no more radio. He hurried away, leaving a desolate silence behind him.

"Somebody out there must have clued him," moaned Sidney finally. "Umar, what do you bet."

"No more Friday-night radio." Martha scowled to keep back tears. "And what if Assad finds out?"

"Well, *Mustapha* won't tell, that's for sure," said Jessica.

Gib exhaled loudly. "I told you there'd be nothing to hear," he said. Weak with disappointment, Matt leaned his head against the wall. "Didn't I?" Gib's voice, following him even into this moment of despair. He ignored it. "Matt, I'm talking to you. How do you like it that your father doesn't think they should negotiate to get us home? How's *that,* after all your big talk about Washington's super negotiator?"

Slowly Matt opened his eyes, peering through the growing dark at his brother, who now stood in the middle of the room. *You're disappointed, too, Gib* — that's what he should say. He stood. "Shut the hell up," he said.

Jessica's voice. "Hey, you guys —"

Sidney's — quick, too tense: "Your dad's right. If you agree to talk to terrorists —"

Gib's again, Gib's face looming nearer now. "Don't tell me to shut up, you SOB. I'm sick of seeing your shining face, always waiting for your fabulous father to save everything, thinking he and you are going to save the world together. Well, you're nothing but a pompous little fart, and he's a big one."

This has been coming forever, Matt thought. I may never understand why. Acting on their own, his shoulders and one foot had braced themselves against the wall, and now he pushed off from it.

He hit Gib hard in the chest and they crashed backward. He felt Gib's head hit the far wall — heard the sickening thud, the broken breath — but Gib's hands were already wrapped in the front of his thobe, and before he could tear them loose he was slammed sideways to the floor. He rolled face-down to get clear — bumping into someone, shoving someone, scrambling to his knees again. He could hear shouts — Jessica's, Sidney's — but they did not matter. He was tuned to no words except Gib's: "Get up, you goddamn phony, get up."

He clambered up, an elbow high for protection, but a fist he never even saw plowed into his stomach. Then, as he instinctively lowered his arms, another exploded in his face — and now at last he was enraged, angry enough to rush Gib with his weight well placed, angry enough to remember coldly everything he had ever been told about fighting — by Gib, it might have been.

He landed a punch solidly where Gib's nose should be, deflected one coming at his own, lunged and lost his balance, and took his brother down with him as he fell.

They scrambled for position. Gib knocked away his support arm, flattening him, and sprawled across his chest; but Matt got an elbow around his brother's neck and a good grip on a wrist, twisted into a better position, and held tight.

Sweat stung his eyes, and he tasted blood. Now neither of them spoke. Straining to keep his hold, Matt heard only the scuffling for position, the tight gasping for breath — and finally, from a great distance, Jessica's voice shouting. "Mustapha! Mustapha!"

They were still tangled on the floor with Gib's elbow jammed against his face when the guards arrived, kerosene lantern swinging, and pulled them apart, all shouting a torrent of Arabic. Mustapha, when the light hit him, looked terrified; the young Sadik looked embarrassed, as though he had seen something he shouldn't have. For a moment Matt saw Steven's face — pale and betrayed.

Someone helped him sit up against the wall. Everything looked strange in the flickering light from the lantern. Would he ever really get his breath again? He closed his eyes and concentrated on it. Someone wiped his face with a wet cloth and then made him hold another one against his cut mouth.

Eventually the guards stood back. Now Matt could see Gib sitting against the opposite wall, panting. His nose looked swollen. Good.

Mustapha held out a rope and demonstrated his question: Would he tie their wrists for the night? Or would they behave?

They nodded; they would behave.

Later, lying in the dark, Matt turned carefully, trying to find a position that didn't put weight on a tender place. The fight was not of his choosing; he would not lie here and feel bad about it now. But he knew that for everyone it had made a terrible evening worse. He remembered the look on Steven's face, and shifted position again to escape it.

Next to him, where he had expected silence, Gib spoke softly. "You never said anything. How come?"

"While we were fighting? Are you kidding? You were the one with so much to say."

A pause. "I kept waiting for you to say something. What would you have said, if you'd said something?"

"Man, what a dumb question." Yes — but there was something important and vulnerable underneath; and without understanding, Matt obeyed its claim on him. "I suppose I'd have said, 'Shut up, you rotten stinking goddamn bastard.' Or maybe something worse."

A chuckle. "Well, yeah. I guess you would."

It seemed to Matt that behind the stupid question and its stupid answer some other question and answer had had their turn, too. His heart swelled suddenly, and in silence he finished his message: *You rotten stinking goddamn bastard — can't you see how much I've always loved you?*

For a while there were only the sounds of breathing, of turning. The swelling over his cheekbone throbbed. Then he heard a soft sobbing, and through it Jessica's crumpled voice: "You dumb, stupid guys. You make me so sick. Who needs terrorists? Who needs kidnapers? You two could louse up the whole world, all alone."

Ten

In the morning Matt could open only one eye, and his split lip was too tender to eat with. "For Pete's sake, stop touching it," said Jessica. "You'd better keep it clean. Lord knows what they do around here if something gets infected."

"You look terrible," said Gib from across the room.

Matt studied him for a moment. "So do you, I'm glad to say." Staring back, Gib suddenly grinned.

There was a little cleaning water left from yesterday. The brothers put on their dirty jeans and scrubbed the spatterings of blood out of their robes.

"It's interesting," said Sidney, watching them work. "The guards call that shirt thing a *thobe*, but Fuad says it like *this*" — he repeated the word, doing something more complicated to the vowel sound — "and the others laugh at him."

"How can you tell all that?" asked Martha.

"I listen, dummy. There are other words, too, that Fuad and Khaled say differently. And some of their words the guards don't recognize at all. Then they all argue till they understand."

"Why do they speak the same language at all, if they're from different countries?"

"Lots of countries use Arabic, but I guess they must all have their own versions."

"Knock, knock." Martha looked around for a taker.

Steven sat straighter. "Who's there?"

"Thobe."

"Thobe who?"

"You've been tho bad I think I'll thpank you," said Martha, bubbling into laughter while the others groaned.

"Oh, vicious," said Gib. "Martha, that's terrible." But Martha kept laughing anyway.

Breakfast seemed late. They lay waiting in silence. Matt could feel their braver mood seeping away. "I wonder if Assad's found out about last night," mused Gib glumly. "If so, everything may hit the fan around here today."

"No more radio," mourned Jessica. "No more news about what's going on back home."

"If the news is like what we heard last night, who needs it?" Sidney seemed to be studying the bones of his toes.

Even Martha's jauntiness seemed affected. "Maybe we're going to sit here *forever*. With nothing to do except watch the fights." She sneaked a sly glance at Matt and Gib through blond eyelashes.

When breakfast finally came, they were sure there was trouble: it was a surly Umar, not Mustapha, who brought it. Umar came at lunch, too, and by then they had noticed other ominous changes. Only one of the work crews had gone to the wadi, and the guards who stayed behind hung around in small groups, watching for Assad to emerge from his hut.

"Mustapha must really be *getting* it," said Martha, kneeling at the front window with her chin on a fist.

"I bet it's not just that radio." Gib's tone was grim. "*Something's* got this whole place tighter than a drum."

"The news!" Jessica's eyes widened. "Maybe they've heard about the U.S. response! It would be bad news to them, too."

"Maybe Assad will tell us," said Martha. "Here he comes."

Assad scowled down at them over folded arms. "So. Maybe by now you know you are in trouble."

"We don't understand," said Jessica. "Why isn't Mustapha bringing our food today?"

Assad snorted. "You *know* why! Because he lets you listen to evil Western music, of course. With my personal radio. Music that even makes you fight, which disturbs Fuad very much. No. Mustapha spoils you, and now he is punished for it — but that is a little thing. You are in trouble for a big thing.

"The U.S. does not care about you. They will not bother to reply to our demands. No reply at all. They do not even say, 'Good-bye, children, sorry.' You must blame your own country, not us, for what will happen to you now. We will have instructions from the za'im soon. Meanwhile, just sit and think how much your country cares about you." The door crashed loudly behind him.

"Bastard," growled Sidney.

"Oh, wow," said Jessica. "Oh, man."

"I don't feel so good," murmured Steven.

"Wait a minute." Matt tried to think. "Sure, this is a setback for them, but there's got to be more going on diplomatically. No way would Washington really leave us out on a limb."

"Besides," said Gib, "we know Assad likes to talk tough."

Matt nodded. "There's no way Tawbah'd give up so soon. That would be stupid. Everybody's just jockeying for position before they talk. Let's stay cool."

But it was impossible not to respond to the tension of the camp and not to dread visits from Umar, who slapped food on the table (Martha said) as though he was mad that it wasn't poison.

By suppertime they could barely touch the bowl. Steven wouldn't even come to the table. "My breathing's not so good today," he explained. "I'll just work on that."

Outside, guards still clustered in twos and threes, arms folded, watching Assad's hut. "He's got high-powered radio stuff in there, I'll bet," said Gib. "That's where he sits and talks to the za'im. That's why the guards are waiting."

"So, stop watching," said Jessica. "Let's not sit here and scare ourselves silly. Martha, come play pebble checkers with me."

But neither of them could keep at it. "Why hasn't Umar come for the supper bowl?" asked Martha, pushing her own pebbles away. "I'm sick of smelling that stuff."

Umar did not come for the bowl until after the sunset prayers, and then he grunted in disgust. He would not carry away such a shamefully full bowl; one of them must carry it out to be emptied. He gestured for Sidney to pick it up. "Maybe someone else better go instead," murmured Gib, starting to rise.

No, the scornful hand indicated; it was to be Sidney. Sidney got slowly to his feet, looking around helplessly. Matt moved to the window to watch as Umar led him toward the ravine and out of sight.

"God, I wish he'd leave Sidney alone," said Matt. "If Sidney stumbles now, with that bowl, he'll make a federal case of it."

They waited in tense silence, listening. For a long time there was only the noise of crickets. Matt rested his head in his arms so he would not have to watch Jessica's taut face, Gib's fingers kneading his forehead, Steven's eyes wider than Matt had ever seen them before — staring blankly at the closed door. At last he lifted his head; there were steps returning.

Once inside, Sidney leaned against the door, shaking violently, but motioning for silence till he was sure it was safe. "They're going to kill us! Tonight! In a few minutes. One by one, when we think he's just taking us on latrine trips."

"What? Oh, God!"

"How do you know?"

"He acted it all out. He even showed me where they'll do it, and throw our bodies in the ravine."

"Oh, don't say that," said Steven. The words seemed shaken out of him. "Take it back, Sidney. Please, take it back."

"Wait a minute." Matt struggled against the sudden flood of panic. "Why would he *tell* you? That doesn't make any sense."

"I don't know. But he liked doing it. You should see how he smiled, watching my face."

"Is that what Assad was telling the guards out there?" cried Martha. "Were they planning?" Then, running to the window, "Where are they? Where did they all go? There's only Umar and two others there now."

"No," said Jessica. "No. We can't let it happen."

"We've got only a few minutes." Sidney pounded his fists against his head. "We have to think of something fast. If only we could get a gun!"

"All right." Gib jumped to his feet in sudden decisiveness. "Martha, stay at the window and tell us when Umar starts this way. Now listen, everyone. Our only chance is to get a weapon. When Umar comes to take the first person, we'll have to jump him. We can do it; there are enough of us. If he has his gun, we'll get it. If he doesn't, at least we can get his knife."

"But the other guards will see it happen!" cried Jessica.

118

"Not if we do it inside." Gib's eyes devoured the room. "We have to figure out how to get him to come in here. Far enough in so that one of us can be behind the door and jump him from the back. Matt, you do that. Then Sidney and Jess, you land on him, too, one on each arm. Martha, stay where you are and shut the door as soon as Matt jumps. I'll go for his knife and stab him."

Jessica gasped. "Do you know how?"

"I'll learn fast. Lord, I hope he brings his gun, too. Then we'll have two weapons."

"We'll have to keep him from yelling," said Sidney. "I'll take off my robe and be ready to smother his face in it."

"But how do we get him in here?" Matt scarcely recognized his own voice.

Gib clutched at the top of his head. "I don't know."

"Tell him there's something scary in here," said Martha. "A big lizard or a rat or something. Behind the table."

"Yeah," said Gib. "That might do it."

"But after that." Matt shook his head, trying to make his brain work faster. "If we — if it works. What do we do next?"

"I don't know yet," said Gib. "But we'll be alive, and we'll have a weapon. The truck! We'll have to get to the truck."

"But we don't have the key! And they'd shoot the tires out if we did!"

"Look out, look out," warned Martha from the window. "Umar's standing up. He's still talking, but he's looking this way."

Gib crouched against the wall. "Get ready. Matt, behind the door. Marth, where you are. When he gets close, you call to him about the rat. No, make it a big scorpion. Jess, over here where you can grab his other arm. Okay, everyone . . ."

Matt jumped to his position, amazed that his muscles would

obey him. He leaned his head back against the wall, to steady it. Then, when the others had taken their positions and frozen into silence, he registered a strange noise — a coarse, uneven rasp.

"Steven!" gasped Jessica. "Look at Steven!"

The child sat fighting for breath, his face the color of his robe, his eyes wide. The pinched sound from his throat was terrifying. "Oh, God," moaned Matt. "Stevie, are you okay?"

The younger boy's eyes swept once across his face, but there was no sound except the dreadful effort to breathe.

"Marth — Umar?" Gib gestured his question.

"He's still just standing there, talking."

Jessica ran to Steven. "What should we do?"

Gib stared. "Is he breathing at all?"

Steven's whole body was shaking now. He arched his chest forward; his hands clenched and unclenched. Martha gave a whispered wail. "Stevie, don't. Someone *do* something!"

"There isn't time!" Sidney gasped.

Matt moved toward the boy, tried to think. "Maybe if we held him up on his feet —"

"I don't think he could stand," said Jessica.

"No time!" cried Gib. "Here, help him sit straighter —"

"I can't stand it!" Martha put her hands over her ears, her own eyes horrified. "Help him! Doesn't anybody know —"

The clash of the bar interrupted her, and she jerked back against the wall in terror. Umar stood staring in, frowning at them all, then squinting harder toward the stricken child.

Matt froze. For a moment there was no movement except for Steven's shaking, no sound except his terrible struggle for air. Then Umar took two steps backward and shouted over his shoulder. "Damn, damn," whispered Gib.

Matt sank numbly to his knees in front of Steven. The boy's

wide eyes caught his, and held. "It's okay, buddy," Matt said automatically, knowing it wasn't true, knowing too that now there was nothing else to say, to do. "Easy, man, easy."

The same despairing quiet seemed to fall over Jessica. "Stevie, Stevie, I was supposed to take care of you." She slipped her shoulder behind his head to cushion it. "I have you now. See, I'm holding you."

Assad and several guards arrived at the door. "What's wrong?"

"It's asthma," Gib answered. "We don't know what to do."

Steven's eyes were still on Matt's face. "Easy, Steve," Matt murmured. "We're all here. It's okay." After a moment he glanced back at Assad. Suddenly his mind sharpened into clarity, and his heart leaped in response; what he saw in Assad's face was worry. *Steven's asthma would not worry Assad if they were all about to be killed.*

"Listen!" said Jessica. "Isn't he getting more air? I think he is! Good, Steven, good. Oh, that sounds better."

They waited. Bit by bit, the fierce sound was easing. The arching of his back subsided, his eyes looked less terrified; he *was* getting new air in. Matt allowed himself a deeper breath. Jessica slipped her shoulder farther behind Steven and began to rock him gently. Martha leaned her forehead against her knees; Sidney slumped against the wall, his face hidden.

When it seemed certain that Steven was recovering, Assad came closer. "Why did this happen, this asthma? Tell me."

Matt groped to invent something. Astonishingly, it was Steven's hoarse voice that answered first. "Umar."

Once more Matt froze. Beside him, Gib started to speak.

"What? Umar? Ssst!" With an angry sweep of his hand Assad silenced Gib and turned back to Steven. "What do you mean?"

121

"Umar says — you'll kill us. Please — don't."

"What?" Assad scanned the faces of the others. "Is this true?" He pointed to Martha. "You say. Speak!"

Martha nodded weakly. "He showed Sidney how you'll throw our bodies in the ravine. Tonight. We've been so scared."

Rapid changes of thought were reflected in Assad's face. Finally he strode to the door, snarled something to the men waiting there, turned back. "Umar is not obedient," he said through tight lips. "Even to the za'im. He will be disciplined. Also, he will not be your guard again."

He looked down at Steven and spoke more calmly. "You will not be killed. Umar lies. Tonight the za'im has said it; we will change nothing. Your government is — what do you say? — bluffing. Tawbah is in control; Tawbah can wait."

He was gone. The room was quiet. Matt sat hunched down, listening to Steven's breathing improve. Sidney lay on his stomach, his face in the crook of an elbow. "We're alive," he said finally, his voice broken and muffled. "It wasn't true. I should feel great. How come I feel so lousy?"

Matt patted his own chest, slowly, as though to train his heart to beat reasonably again. "That was too close," he said.

"Wow, Steven," said Martha. "You really had us wiped out. Would you please try not to do that again?"

Steven had slid away from Jessica and was sitting alone against the wall. Matt couldn't make out his expression. "I'm sorry," he said quietly. "I couldn't help it. I tried."

Gib, leaning thoughtfully on an elbow, gave a long, toneless whistle. "Don't apologize. Think about it, everyone. If Stevie hadn't had that attack, what would we have done to Umar? Or tried to do? Matt's right; we couldn't have gotten away from here. So what do you suppose might have happened to us then? I think you saved us, Steve. I think your old asthma saved us. From one hell of a lot of trouble."

"Oh," moaned Sidney. "I feel *terrible*. Does anybody feel good?"

"Not me," said Jessica. "Not yet."

"Too close," Matt whispered. "Oh, God, too close."

Eleven

Even having Mustapha appear with breakfast the next morning did not lift the heaviness that lay over them. Only Steven seemed really hungry. "We almost made a colossal mistake," said Jessica when they were alone again. "That's why we're so bummed out. But we were terrified; we thought we were going to be killed in a few minutes; we had to decide very fast what to do."

"It sure is a lousy way to make decisions," said Matt, shaking his head to jar loose the memory.

"We were going to kill Umar," whispered Martha, her eyes wide. "That's amazing. We were really dangerous, weren't we? And stupid."

They sat in glum silence for a few minutes. Gib was slowly smoothing a place on the ground with his bare heel. Finally he looked around at everyone. "There's one thing that was right about last night — we began to help ourselves. We made a mistake, and we were damned lucky it didn't screw everything up, but — for the first time we began to work to save ourselves."

"Hey, yeah," said Sidney. "That's right."

"And I think that's what we're going to *have* to do. Matt

124

thinks negotiations just haven't started yet. But, look — how far can the U.S. get against demands like those, anyway? I don't pin too many hopes on talks. As for being rescued — the Marines certainly can't come for us if they don't know where we are. Somebody watch the windows."

Sidney and Jessica jumped to the assignment. Matt, too, felt a sudden chill of excitement. "So what do we do?" Sidney prompted.

"I'm not sure yet. Maybe we can escape. Anyway, we'll have to start by learning a lot more about where the heck we are."

"From the guards, you mean?" Jessica looked dubious. "Assad said we're not allowed to ask that kind of question."

"I mean from studying things. Like that little jet we've seen a couple of times. What's it doing here in the middle of nowhere? Who could it belong to? And using our brains about where we could be. Damn, we've got to find a way to get outside more. We've got to start figuring out if we can rescue ourselves."

"Are you serious?" asked Matt. "You seriously think we could get ourselves out of here without getting blown away?"

"I seriously think we'd better start working on it."

Sidney slapped the wall. "Hey. All right! Now you're talking. Now we're going to start turning this thing around!"

"Mm, good, Sidney," said Jessica, mocking him a little. "Just what do you suggest we do first?"

Rebuffed, he frowned at the wall. "Well, to begin with, you might change that dumb drawing. I'm tired of looking at Adam's hand, hanging there like a dead fish. Let him make a fist. That can be our symbol that we're through just lying around."

Matt shook his head. "Let's not talk about drawing fists on

125

the wall. It's not a question of power; it's a question of smarts. And there's no way we'll get anywhere unless we really make Assad trust us."

Gib nodded. "Right. We're going to have to outthink them. We lie low, we observe, we behave like good little hostages — and we see how far we can get with it."

Jessica checked her window. "Cool it, everyone. Here comes a delegation. Assad and Fuad both."

But Assad entered the room alone. "Fuad sends you two messages," he said. "First, as a good Bedu host, he apologizes for Umar's bad behavior. He agrees that Umar shall not speak to you again.

"The second message is for the brothers." He looked at Matt and Gib. "He says it is a bad thing that you fight. Brothers are *khamsa*; they should defend each other, not fight. I tell him it is the fault of the Western music, but he believes you fight because you are in this room, like a cage. It is the way of Islam to be kind, even to prisoners. We have decided to let all you boys help to build the dikes. So you will not need to fight. Of course, the guards will like it better this way, too."

Matt listened soberly, avoiding the other hostages' eyes.

"Since Mustapha is working on the dikes, too, maybe Martha and I can help with the cooking," offered Jessica quickly.

"No. Mustapha works there only a few hours. He will still fix the food." He turned back to the boys, frowning. "You will always be under close watch, and the guards will be armed. If anyone makes trouble, he will be severely punished. And everyone will be locked up again. Permanently."

He stood up. "So. Tomorrow you will begin. You must work barefoot. Unless we can find some sandals for you; I will see."

He stopped at the door. For a moment the disdainful mask

slipped from his face. "There is fresh food. Tonight you will have chicken."

When he was safely gone, they exploded into soundless whoops of delight. "It's happening already!" crowed Gib in a hoarse whisper. "Oh, *man*, will we cooperate!" Then his smile faded. "Steven, thank God for your asthma."

That night they did indeed feast on chicken stew, olives, and goat's milk. And a breathtaking new hope. After they ate, Jessica redrew Adam's hand. Now the down-turning fingers were not limp but taut and eager, and they were reaching for a hammer.

"Not a hammer, you turkey," said Sidney, chuckling. "You don't build a dike with a hammer."

"With what, then?"

"A trowel," said Matt. "For cement. Like a bricklayer uses." So Jessica drew a mason's trowel, just within Adam's reach.

As it turned out, there was no use for trowels in building the dikes. No water meant no cement. In fact, the hostages were not permitted to use what tools there were, the picks and shovels. But Matt didn't care. Just being out of his prison, being allowed to work hard and grow tired from it would have been relief enough; the secret goal of planning toward freedom at the same time shook his insides with fear and joy.

That first morning, the wind changed; the dust-heavy air from the desert vanished before a fresh breeze from the north, and the rock was cool under Matt's feet as he emerged from the hut. Assad handed Gib a pair of worn sandals for the older boys to share.

There were three work crews of five or six men each, many of whom stared in curiosity at the hostages. Matt was glad to see two friendly faces — Mustapha's creased and grinning,

Sadik's smooth and serious as he nodded a greeting. There was no sign of Umar.

Khaled, the supervisor, assigned Matt and Gib to separate crews, Sidney and Steven to the third. They all set out in the direction of the desert, along the ravine. Matt picked his footing carefully along the rocky path, which passed between sharp peaks and inclines. Eventually it opened out above a brief stretch of low land, with another wall of rock rising beyond.

Now Matt could see where their work lay. Here the ravine emptied into a narrow valley floor with a sandy bottom. Along the center of the valley ran a shallow depression perhaps thirty feet wide, where he could see a few signs of vegetation: the flattened remains of something like tumbleweed, a small dead bush of gray branches. And this poor little stretch of land had provided — would provide again, if the rains came — grain for how many Bedu families? Standing there, brushing one tender sole against the calf of his other leg, Matt wondered for the first time about the people who really lived in this dead place.

The foreman of his crew — Abou, a slight young man with surprising blue eyes — showed Matt the work. Today they were to start another of the low stone dikes that would reach out across the wadi. One worker, using a long-handled spade, would dig a trough in the sand for bedding the rocks; one would set the rocks into the trough; two would bring rocks from the foot of the cliffs by dragging them on what turned out to be the upside-down fender of an old car. And apparently there would always be a crew member standing guard from higher ground, rifle at hand.

Matt watched as several guards got ready for work by tucking the rear hems of their robes up into the front of their belts, leaving their bare legs free. This arrangement looked very sensible, and he copied them. Abou showed him how to wrap strips of rag around his hands, to serve as work gloves.

He set to work teamed with a stranger — loading rocks onto the fender sledge, gathering up its rope slings, leaning forward as their feet dug into the sand until the sledge began to slide. It could have been brutally hard work, but the loose, light-colored clothing seemed to protect Matt from the sun, and there were frequent rest breaks. His swollen eye no longer bothered him, but the cut lip soon began to throb, and the soles of his feet smarted.

Finally Abou raised a hand high and called the crew to lunch. Matt tried squatting like the others, but soon gave up and sat cross-legged, waiting eagerly for the packets of bread and dates that passed from hand to hand around the circle, for the goatskin bags of water that followed. He had never actually eaten with Arabs before. Tearing off bites of bread, he stole curious glances at these men who ate and talked, ignoring him. They were his captors, and might still become his executioners; but since this morning they had become something else: his partners in construction. It blurred his sense of the vast gulf between him and them, and made him uneasy.

He reached for another date. Instantly Abou barked at him, making him snatch back his hand. What was wrong? Beneath Abou's horrified expression, the slender hands demonstrated: Matt had reached for food with his left hand, and that was not allowed. He must eat with his right hand only.

The Arabs were obviously shocked. Matt felt ashamed — and then annoyed. Why be ashamed for breaking a rule he had never been taught? The shame was a trick — his head giving in to his captivity, keeping him helpless. Being annoyed was better.

Always, traps. Terror was one kind of trap; feeling helpless, ashamed, was another. That's why Sidney kept talking about resistance. Watching the Arabs begin their midday prayers, Matt thought about this: if the captives were going to work toward their own freedom, they would have to keep their minds secretly confident — secretly, fiercely free.

For the rest of the afternoon Matt worked as the rock-placer. This job was interesting; he liked choosing rock faces that could be fit most closely together or overlapped most efficiently. Stooping tired him, but by changing position frequently he could rest his back.

By the end of the day, all the boys were exhausted. Back in the hut Mustapha clicked his tongue at how quickly they emptied the dinner bowl, and he brought them an extra pot of sweet tea. For the first time the girls had been excluded from the outside adventure, and they listened eagerly to details of the work.

Finally, when Mustapha had left for the last time, Gib sent Steven and Martha to watch at the windows. "Okay. What did we *learn?*"

Matt groaned. "How not to eat with your left hand. How to tuck up your thobe so you can work better. How to wrap your hands so you can lift sandy rocks without ruining your fingerprints. Geez, the rocks are bad enough, but the sand makes them murder!"

Gib grimaced. "Nothing else?"

Matt grew thoughtful. "Well, there's no chance of escaping from there. Every crew always has one guy watching us."

"Not just *us*, though," added Sidney. "They keep looking around, too — to make sure the Marines aren't creeping up on 'em."

"Yeah — but I'm beginning to think they're not really expecting a rescue attempt at all," said Gib, hugging one knee.

130

"Jess, how many guards did you see today, while we were gone?"

"Just the two at the main post. And Mustapha, at lunch."

"That's what I figured. I think there are a total of maybe twenty guys here. You girls have seen tents to the north, but I sure didn't see any today on the desert side. Did anybody?" No, nobody had. "Now, twenty guys is maybe enough to keep us in line, but it's nothing to use against a U.S. rescue force."

Matt was intrigued. "So?"

"So I think they're pretty sure there won't *be* any rescue attempts. Because no one but them knows where we are. I think they figure this is a very unlikely place, a million miles from where anyone expects us to be. Look how relaxed they act — letting us out to work, never more than a few guards on duty near us, radios going at night, everything. I think they're delighted with themselves for leaving no trail behind."

"Speaking of radios, *we* saw something today," said Jessica. "Coming back with water we walked a little closer to Assad's hut, and you can see a couple of wires running from the back of it up higher over the rocks. Antennas, I'll bet."

Gib nodded. "That follows. That's what brings the bad news of no news every night."

"From where, though?" asked Matt. "From the za'im, or that Yussef guy — but where the heck are they?"

Gib shook his head. "Doesn't matter, as long as they're too far to send reinforcements fast. When Assad needs them."

Jessica leaned forward. "And when will that be?"

Gib checked Steven and Martha at the windows, then looked back at the others. "When the Marines land. After they find out where we are. Which is after *we* find that out, and tell 'em."

Matt grunted skeptically. "Great. How do we do that?"

"We'll have to smuggle the information out somehow. But the first thing is figuring out where we are, and we've started on that already. We know, roughly, the directions of the compass from here. Let's see what else we know. Everybody shut your eyes. Now — point in the direction you think the truck came from when it brought us here. Hold it — and open your eyes." They looked around at each other. "Not bad. Everybody's pointing mostly north — maybe northeast or northwest, but generally north. When the wind is from the south, it's full of dust. Desert to the south. Today it was from the north, and it was fresh and clear. If we're right about where the truck came from, and if the fresh breeze means anything, the Mediterranean must be to the north of us."

"Today you could smell it," said Steven, at the window.

"What?" Gib was excited. "Are you sure, Stevie?"

"Oh, yes. Every time I'd get up on a really high place, looking for rocks. That salty smell. It was really nice."

"Hey — here's something else to prove it!" Sidney hit the side of his head as though he should have thought of this earlier. "When the guards pray toward Mecca, they really do face east!"

Matt frowned. "So? Mecca *is* to the east, isn't it?"

"Not from everywhere. From Israel and Lebanon and places like that it would be a lot more south than east."

They stared at him. "Draw it," said Gib. "On the floor. But very lightly; we'll have to rub it off. You two on the windows, stay sharp. For gosh sake, don't let anyone creep up on us now."

They watched as Sidney drew the Mediterranean Sea and indicated Israel, Syria, Lebanon, Saudi Arabia. "Mecca's in

Saudi Arabia, somewhere real near the Red Sea. Maybe about here. So if the guards face east, we must be somewhere here. Like Gib said." He indicated the whole sweeping coast of northern Africa.

"So, what countries would that be?" asked Jessica. "Go on, Sidney, you're doing fine."

Sidney stared at the map for a minute. "Well, this part is Egypt, just across the Red Sea. But I'm not sure I remember the rest. The farther you get from Israel, the less I know."

Gib put a finger on Egypt. "Okay, we could be here, in this part of Egypt. Mediterranean to the north, Mecca to the east. Or any of these other North African countries. Anybody else know what they are?"

Nobody did. "Oh, man," moaned Matt. "Algeria's somewhere there. And Morocco. But where? And what else? The whole top of the continent — and I can't remember."

"This is awful," said Jessica, her voice tight with frustration. "Assad is right. We *are* ignorant." They looked down at the map, avoiding each other's eyes. Again Matt felt shame, and a returning undertow of helplessness.

"Well, so what?" Gib gestured angrily. "Does being a little ignorant mean we're stupid, too? Maybe we'll remember more tomorrow. Meanwhile, we don't have to know the *name* of where we are to know a lot about it. Mediterranean to the north, desert to the south. How would you describe the terrain?"

Matt struggled away from the undertow. "Barren mountains. All one kind of rock — sort of greenish gray. It must be pretty soft stuff — I saw lots of caves and fissures today."

Gib nodded. "Limestone, or something like that."

"And we know the mountains must come pretty close to the coast," Matt went on. "Remember that horrible ride in the truck? A bumpy road on flat land for just a little while, and then *ages* of climbing. Turning, twisting, going slow."

Gib was still nodding. "How long would you say that trip took?"

Jessica sighed. "It seemed like forever."

"Yeah," said Martha from the window, "but it really couldn't have been more than five or six hours. I *never* could go longer than that, when I'm awake, without having to go to the bathroom. I mean, I'd had a big drink on the boat, and everything."

"Okay, good! So — five or six hours. With a lot of winding and climbing slowly on a terrible road. So the straight-line distance from here to the coast is maybe less than fifty miles."

"Maybe a *lot* less," said Matt, "because of all that twisting back and forth when we were climbing."

"Right," added Sidney. "And Steven can smell the salt water, don't forget. How far away do you suppose that means?"

No one was sure; but it did seem encouraging.

"Okay," said Gib. "Rub out the map, for now. Next subject — what do we know about the people who live around here? Pretend we could telephone out of here to some experts on northern African countries. What clues could we give them about the local people?"

"Not much," said Matt. "After all, most of the guards are foreigners, like us. Maybe from a lot of different places."

"But Fuad and Khaled?"

"Well, okay." Matt leaned forward. "They're Beduins. Their particular tribe wears gray kaffiyehs with braided black ties."

"Some of them keep sheep or goats," said Jessica. "Marth and I've seen them. Besides, we often get fresh goat's milk."

"And when the rainy season starts, some of them move their flocks south, closer to the desert, and try to raise barley in the wadis." Gib's voice was excited.

134

Matt shook his head thoughtfully. "For all we know that might be true of half the Beduin tribes in the world."

"So — keep going."

Sidney took it up. "We know Fuad and Khaled use some Italian words. Now that seems odd. What Arabs south of the Mediterranean would know some Italian? That might be a real clue."

Jessica caught her breath. "And, Sidney, you said there are differences in their Arabic, that the others can't understand —"

"Oh, right!" Gib's eyes were shining. "Those could be some of the best clues of all! Sidney, you've gotta start listening for all the differences you can possibly pick up."

"Hey, yeah!" Sidney slapped his knees with excitement. "Well, like today! Khaled said something to the guards about the 'gerba,' but they didn't know what he meant until he showed it to them. He meant our water bag. Things like that —"

"Exactly. *Now* we're cooking."

Martha, kneeling by the window, turned to look at them. "But we *can't* telephone any experts. So what good is that stuff?"

Gib relaxed back against the wall. "We'll let you know when we get it all figured out, Martha baby."

She looked out into the fading light once more. "I'd rather know simple stuff. Like what country we're in."

For a minute they sat, listening to a cricket tuning up. Then Gib said, "A license plate. That might clue us about what country we're in. Maybe the truck has one."

Jessica shook her head. "It doesn't. I looked for it the day we got here." She shrugged at their surprise. "Instinct. My mother always said, get the license number."

135

"Nice try," said Matt. The cricket was working hard. Soon it would be sunset and time for the guards' prayers.

"I saw an old, junked car today," said Steven. "It didn't have a license plate, either. It didn't even have a battery, and it was all full of sand."

"Where, Stevie?" asked Gib.

"A hidden place, down behind where I was working. I bet the guards don't even know about it. The car's been there for a long time. It's real old-fashioned, with big, curvy fenders."

"How did you happen to find it?"

"I saw it from high up." He looked around; they were all listening to him. "See, my job is to go by myself high up in the cliffs and find smaller rocks for the dikes. Bakhit — that's my boss — he showed me how to slide them partway down, and make piles. I found millions. Bakhit told me I did a good job."

Martha checked the window again. "Better watch it now. The guards are coming up."

"Okay," said Gib, stretching. "Not bad, for the first run. See, you guys? See how much we know?"

Matt and Steven helped Sidney rub out the last traces of the map. Then they dipped out a little wash water and cleaned their hands. Matt glanced at Steven. "So, who's this Bakhit?"

"My boss. I scraped my knee on a rock, and he put a bandage on it. See?"

Matt inspected the tidy cloth wrap. "And Bakhit told you you did a good job, huh? Not in English. How did he tell you that?"

"With his face," answered Steven, casually enough — but a flush of pride spread over his own.

Later, lying down to sleep, Steven wrapped himself carefully in his blanket. Exhaustion was making him shiver with cold. It was good to be so tired, though; it meant he ought to sleep quickly tonight.

For several nights now, he had lain awake late, thinking of home. At first, he would imagine what he and his parents would do to celebrate when he got home. As long as he could think of the three of them together, the home thoughts were okay.

But the last few nights he had not been able to keep from wondering about his parents right now. He kept imagining them alone in the house and silent, without him to talk to and to discuss with each other, without his health to worry about. Of course, they would be worrying about his *safety*, now; but would it be a together-worry, where they might comfort each other, or a fight-worry, where they would blame each other? In his imagination, they never wanted to sit next to each other on the living room sofa, where their knees might touch; instead, one always sat alone, while the other stood, turned away, looking out a window.

He was ashamed that when the others talked wistfully of home his own troubled thoughts kept him silent.

But tonight would be different. On this astonishing day he had done hours of work with strange men on bare hills, and the muscles in his body tingled to prove it. "Good night," he thought hastily toward home. "I love you." Already his mind was floating toward sleep; again he was seeing stones.

Matt listened to the other boys' breathing deepen and steady as they dropped off to sleep — Steven first, Sidney soon after,

137

then Gib. Sleep was coming so easily tonight. Fuad had been more on target than he knew; working in the wadi was very good for them. For the first time since the kidnaping, they had been glad for night. It was wonderful to be worn out.

From behind the curtain he could hear Martha's noisy breathing — almost a snore. He could not hear Jessica. Was she, also, asleep? Or were she and he the last two awake?

Here they were, only a few feet apart. He hadn't forgotten what it was like to feel her body against his. Had she even noticed that moment? Probably not — they had all been so frightened about Sidney.

When she lay awake at night, like tonight, did she think about him? About Gib? He had been holding his breath, listening for hers; he released it now in a quiet sigh.

Underneath all the tension and excitement of the last few days, he had found himself more steadily aware of her than before. Sometimes he just wanted to sit looking at her for a while. But he seldom allowed himself to, because balancing this new wish was his increased caution about Gib. The Friday-night fight between them had clearly proved that there mustn't be any more of that. Probably the same realization was making Gib cautious, too; it seemed to Matt that since then both of them had been playing it pretty cool with each other, about everything. Including Jessica.

But his night thoughts, his imaginings, were something else again. They were his own business, and no threat to anything at all. Now that even Jessica was asleep — he *could* hear her slow, rhythmic breathing — he was alone with them.

Twelve

The next afternoon, when Matt and the other boys returned from work, Jessica was watching for them at the window. "Some good news and some bad," she said, when they were sure the guards were once more out of earshot. "The good news is they're easing up some already! They left the door unbarred this afternoon, and Assad said we can go to the latrine alone as long as the guards on duty say it's okay. I guess with you guys loose all day, keeping too close a watch on us seemed sort of silly."

Gib tipped himself a cup of water. "The bad news?"

Martha grimaced. "It's my fault. I wanted to help find out where we are. So when Mustapha brought lunch I did this with my hands, all around, and said, 'Mustapha — Egypt?' Then he got real upset and went right to Assad. And now maybe we're in for it."

Sure enough Assad arrived after supper, his frown a storm warning. "I have told you you are not to know details about your detention, and not to ask questions of the guards. It is the ruling of the za'im. If you ask again, there will be severe punishment, and all privileges will be stopped. You understand?" They nodded.

"I'm sorry, Assad," said Martha. "It's just, I got so *bored*."

Assad ignored her. "Men are the governors of their women. In captivity, these women are your sisters. If you cannot control them, it is your shame." He glowered at Gib and Matt.

"We will meet our responsibility," said Gib seriously.

"You'll regret it if you do not."

It sounded like a parting shot; yet Assad stood leaning against the wall, his arms folded. They waited, uncomfortable. Finally he turned to Matt. "Of course, if you behave foolishly, we will not be surprised. That is how your country is behaving."

Matt's heart jumped. Was there news? He dared not ask. "We don't know what the U.S. is doing," he answered carefully.

"It does nothing! Your foolish government still makes no response to our demands. That is stupid! Do they not care for your lives?"

Matt hid his disappointment. Again he chose his answer cautiously. "Perhaps the demands seem too unfair."

"Unfair!" Assad's eyes widened. "The demands are simply for a chance for survival for the world — Muslims, and everyone else. That the U.S. repent for leading the world into this terrible danger and turn away from nuclear arms. That is not 'unfair'!"

Matt heard Sidney breathing heavily and shot him a fast glare. There must be no debate this time; they must find out why Assad had brought this up, and take advantage of it. He waited.

"The za'im knows that many in Congress recognize the guilt of the U.S. for the arms race. Your newspapers report it. I have seen that, many times. Yet your government is silent now, at our demands! It is arrogance."

Careful, careful. "Many Americans do believe we should help lead the way to disarmament. But, to do it alone —"

140

"Your own father believes the U.S. must turn back! He has said so, many times. He has introduced bills. Now his sons are in danger of their lives, now he could say even stronger what he believes is right, and he is silent! The za'im is disgusted."

Matt released his held breath. Astonishing, this knowledge of his father. What to answer? "I don't know why he is silent."

Assad finally looked away. Had he gotten what he came for? Matt had no idea. "Well. The za'im is generous; we will wait a little longer." He straightened. "It is clear. None of you will ask questions. Disobedience will be harshly punished." At the door he looked back at Matt, at Gib. Again the disdainful superiority faded from his face, and Matt could see a strange, wistful appeal in it. "In Washington I have several times heard your father speak about American weapons. At American University. At a foreign student forum. He speaks well." He turned away quickly and clanged the bar into place behind him.

Oh, God, thought Matt, his scalp turning cold with the realization. Is that it? Assad believes in my father the way I do.

In the morning, when Mustapha had left them alone with the bowl of breakfast beans, Gib looked pointedly across the low table at Martha. "Woman, this is your master speaking. No more questions, right?"

Martha twisted her mouth. "Assad never even looked at me last night. Not once. Did you notice? Even when I said I was sorry."

" 'We will meet our responsibilities,' " mimicked Jessica, rolling her eyes sideways at Gib. "Oh, brother."

Gib ignored her. "We've got to think about this. Not that you're a girl, Marth, but that you're young. You and Steven both."

"I'm almost as old as Sidney!"

"You are not," Sidney retorted. "I'm thirteen, you're eleven. That's a big difference."

Gib frowned at the table. "The question is, how can we expect you younger kids to know everything we're doing and keep your mouths shut? There's an awful lot at stake."

"I never told *anything*," said Martha fervently, "and I never would. I just *asked* something. And I won't do that anymore."

"I won't ever tell anything, either," said Steven. "I keep lots of secrets, all the time."

"There's the practical side of it, too, Gib," said Jessica. "How *could* we plan without them? In just the one room?"

Martha's face was bunched like a fist. "Don't you leave us out of anything. We can help, too. Like, did anybody but me notice that the little plane flew south Saturday morning about two hours before lunch, and came back yesterday in the middle of the afternoon? I watch for it from the window, to see if it has a regular schedule. Because that might be a clue."

There was a silence; then Matt whistled into it. "Outa sight, Martha!"

Gib tipped his hand to her. "Okay. We'll do it all together. But everyone's got to be super careful. We'd better work quickly, too. The za'im seems to be getting impatient."

Martha's face eased. "I'll make it up to you guys. You'll see."

That evening and each evening that followed, they posted watch at the windows and eagerly discussed things they had noticed that might become clues to their whereabouts. Sometimes there was discouragingly little to report. Then they cushioned their disappointment by relating the ordinary events of the day. The girls reported seeing a gazelle on their walk to the well. Steven had seen several snakes and scorpions. Gib had seen vultures. Everyone complained of the heat. And always the boys compared notes on the steadily lengthening dikes.

"Sadik and I figured out this great new chute system," said Sidney one evening. "If you find a much more gradual slope for the really *big* suckers, you can get 'em to roll a lot farther out into the wadi. Saves time and muscle."

"Gosh, Sadik actually communicates with you?" asked Jessica. "How did you manage that? He's so shy."

"Oh, we don't talk or anything." Sidney shrugged it off. "We just gesture. But he's okay. He's got some good ideas, and he works hard. It's funny — whenever we've done something really well, he gets this big grin like a little kid, but he always rubs his nose to hide it. I get a kick out of that.

"You other guys can steal our chute system, if you want to."

Slowly their hoard of clues grew. Many evenings Sidney could describe a new distinction between Khaled's local dialect and the Arabic of the others. Martha continued to watch for the little plane. Jessica began to make a drawing of the local terrain, using a tiny twig dipped in wet mud and drawing on the back of a piece of paper from someone's jeans pocket. "Good!" said Gib, watching her work — and leaning closer than necessary, it seemed to Matt. "Put in the huts and tents and the well and the ravine and everything you know about. Then we guys can add the peaks to the south, and the wadi and stuff. That'll be a big help to the Marines."

"We're going to mail it to them, I suppose," said Matt.

143

"But for gosh sakes, keep it hidden, Jess! Under your mat, behind the curtain. It would be the end of us, if they found it."

It was Matt, one day sitting back on his heels to retie the rags around his hands and looking up at a circling hawk, who thought of spy satellites. What if they could construct some kind of signal that would be visible only from the sky? When they discussed it that evening, Steven reported that he knew just the place for it — a remote little peak with a surprising saucer-shaped top, which was hidden from all angles below. He had stretched out there once, for a minute or two, to be hidden from all the world — till the heat drove him down.

They puzzled for some time about what could be put up there. Gib said something reflective would be best. Finally Sidney came up with the answer — hubcaps from the old junked car Steven had found. The only remaining problem was that Steven would have to be relied on to set up the signal by himself. The three older boys were always kept with their crews; only Steven, sent stone-hunting among the higher peaks, was allowed to work alone.

"They think he's too young to cause trouble!" crowed Martha. "I love it! I *told* you older guys we'd help."

Jessica objected. "It scares me. It's so risky for Steven. And what if they find the place?"

"I don't think they ever would," said Steven, "as long as Bakhit doesn't see me climbing up there. I'll be very careful."

"What if they see you carrying the hubcaps?"

"You'll have to be ready with something good, Stevie," said Gib. "Like, you were going to ask Assad if we could put them up in here as decorations, or something. The signal's risky, but it's important. It could be the best idea yet."

They were very careful to seem trustworthy; and the door

144

to the hut was barred less and less. Except for work assignments, they still were allowed out only for trips to the latrine, or to bathe or do laundry behind the hut; but now these errands were permitted with just a call to the guards at the main post. "Fabulous," exulted Gib. "By now nobody expects trouble from us. Keep it up, everyone."

Matt learned more about the little plane, almost without trying. He and his foreman had paused for a drink of water one hot afternoon. Matt held out the goatskin, but Abou didn't see it; he was gazing to the east, where the plane was barely visible in the distance, glinting in the afternoon sun. They watched it for a moment together. On impulse Matt went into a tail-gunner routine, mimicking strafing action and making sound effects through his teeth.

No, no, said Abou's gesture; Matt was all wrong. The little plane was coming from the south, where there was — now one hand made a downward drilling motion, followed by an upward spouting — an oil well. Moreover, the people in the plane were — what? — French! The foreman pinched his face into a supercilious, dandified expression (Peter Sellers, thought Matt first), and his fingers scrabbled under his nose to indicate a tiny mustache. "Paree," he said, as a final clue. "Toujours l'amour."

Matt grinned at the caricature, then reached for the water bag to hide his excitement. A French oil company to the south! That — plus the flight schedule of the company plane — had to be a terrific clue.

But about how they might get these clues to someone who could use them, Gib would say nothing, in spite of their pestering. "Wait till Friday, when we'll have all day to talk."

Friday began on a high note when Sidney came back from bathing. "Oh, man," he exploded softly. "Beerte. Sadik didn't know I'd understand, but I did. Beerte. That's the name of the town where Assad and Fuad go to the mosque. And it's *that* direction." He pointed northwest.

"Are you sure?" Jessica's whisper squeaked with excitement. "If it's got a mosque, it ought to be big enough to be on maps!"

"*All right!*" Matt exclaimed. "Another clue! Let's get going. Steven, you and me on the windows. If anybody comes, we're playing sports trivia. Okay, Gib, shoot."

Gib leaned forward, elbows on knees. "I think pretty soon we'll have enough on this place to clue the experts. I mean, enough stuff that once we get it to them, they can do the rest. And this is how I think we can get it to them.

"I think we can get two people out of here, on foot, heading north toward the coast, and give them about a thirty-hour head start before the guards know they're missing. The two people will be Sidney and me. Me because I've done wilderness camping and because I think fast on my feet. Sid because he's memorized all these dialect clues the rest of us can't even hear, and because he speaks Italian. We travel mostly by night and don't talk to anyone as long as we can avoid it, or until we get a safe chance to ride. *When* we get a ride, or when we have to talk, we're Italian kids, maybe running away from home. Sidney does the talking. I'm his deaf cousin. I'm mute."

"Wait a minute," said Sidney. "Sure, I speak Italian, but I must have an American accent."

"An *Italian* would know that. But would Arabs hear the difference? I doubt it."

"Go on," said Matt. "How about this thirty-hour head start?"

"Okay. The getaway. We know this place is riddled with caves and fissures. Real flatlands would be dangerous, but I'll bet you can go a long way north from here, maybe all the

146

way to the coast, keeping to the rougher areas where it's easy to hide.

"Have you seen those caves below the latrine? There are two little shallow caves that go nowhere, but the third opens out into a fissure that ends up in front of these bluffs the huts are on — out where you can see the guard tents."

"How did you learn all this?" asked Sidney.

Gib grinned. "Long trips to the john. You hadn't noticed? Anyway, from there we travel north by night, swinging way to the east at first to avoid the tents, and staying where the terrain is rough enough to hide in. We leave on a Thursday night."

"But how do you get away?" interrupted Martha.

"We just don't come back from the last latrine trip. Right now, they wave us permission to go but don't bother to check that we come back. So between now and then we've got to be super careful not to give them any reason to get suspicious and start tightening up on those trips."

Matt objected. "But Assad always checks in before the door is barred for the night, to be sure everyone's there. Except Fridays, of course."

"But we *are* all there! Or, we seem to be. Assad never looks beyond the curtain, of course — Allah forbid! — so he won't know the girls' room is empty and the person all wrapped up in a blanket on Sidney's mat is really Martha, and the person on my mat is Jessica."

"Clever," said Jessica. "Clever. But dangerous."

"What about the next day?" asked Matt.

"Not so fast. When Assad sees people curled up for sleep already, somebody tells him that you're not feeling well. Maybe it's something you ate for dinner. It's worse by the next day — which isn't a workday, anyway — and everyone stays in bed. By then Assad and Fuad have left for Friday services, and Mustapha will be glad to stay away from sick people. Nobody wants to eat; Mustapha just brings a pot of tea to the door.

"Now, chances are Mustapha won't even look in late Friday night, before he bars the door. But if he does, there's a body on every mat this side of the curtain, like the night before.

"Anyway, Matt hollers out to the guards early Saturday morning — very early, to be convincing — and says Gib and Sidney have been gone since the night before, and now everyone's afraid they'll get lost and die and will the guards please go find them and bring them safely back. Only it's really been two nights, not one, and we're far, far away."

"Wait a minute," said Jessica. "My head's spinning. Why did you and Sidney run away? I mean, what do we *say* is the reason?"

"Because Matt and I had another terrible fight." Gib grinned; he was proud of this. "And I said I'd kill him, if I stayed — which is a dishonorable thing to do to a younger brother, so I left in a rage. Don't you think that would sound convincing to an Arab?"

"I'm not sure." Matt felt oddly disgruntled. "No *American* would buy it."

"Hey," said Sidney, "what about me? Why did I go with you?"

"Not sure yet. We'll have to work on that."

"*I* know," said Jessica, excited. "To calm Gib down and get him to come back. And the rest of us hoped that would work, and that's why we didn't say anything when Mustapha barred the door at night, because we didn't want both of you to get into trouble. All night long we waited for you to come back,

148

getting more and more scared — and finally we couldn't stand it anymore."

"Perfect!" exclaimed Gib. "You got it, Jessica. Meanwhile, Sid and I are way to the north. We carry bread and dates and goat cheese and two water bags. I've already got one hidden away that nobody's even missed! We travel hard. Straight through, for the first fifteen or sixteen hours, sighting by the stars at night. By early afternoon Friday we should be far enough away to stop and sleep for a few hours, and then go on. By the time you blow the whistle Saturday morning we may be all the way to the coast."

"What happens there?" Matt was torn between admiration for the plan and a mounting sense of foreboding.

"Sidney somehow gets us to a town where there are some Europeans or Americans, and as soon as we're sure we're in friendly company we say who we are and ask for help."

"But what if Assad gets everybody in the country looking for you?" asked Martha.

"He can't. The whole plan hinges on one theory, and I'll bet you anything it's right: nobody but this one little group of twenty men — and the za'im and the other brains of the organization, but they're far away somewhere — nobody else knows that we're here! No way could Assad pull off this desert-prison business with just two dozen men and some rifles if people knew we were here. See what that means? As soon as we've gotten really away from here, and Assad doesn't know where to look for us, we're safe. We're just two Italian kids, on holiday — on our way to getting six American kids home free."

They all sat silent for a moment. Matt looked at Jessica. She, too, seemed increasingly troubled. "I don't know," she said finally. "Even if it all works just the way you say it will, and Assad believes our story, everything will be totally changed here, afterward. We'll all be locked up tighter than ever, helpless again, and — oh, God, Gib — we won't know what's happened to *you*, for ages." Her voice locked shut on her then.

Watching her, Matt felt a strange pain. He made himself think. "She's right, Gib," he said. "That'll be awful. Staying here, losing all the freedom we've won. And we'll have to wonder, all day every day, what's happened to you two. It'll be hell."

"But only for a few days." Gib turned to Jessica. "A week, at most — and then the Marines. This place should be a cinch to take." He was appealing to her, but she wouldn't look up at him. Finally he threw out his hands in frustration. "Look, anyone have a better idea?"

No one spoke.

"We have to take the risks, to get ourselves home. Do you think there's any other way that it's going to happen?"

Finally Jessica answered for all of them. "I guess it's the best chance we've got."

Sidney erupted with a muffled roar of excitement and began shadowboxing the curtain, until Gib barked at him. "Knock it off, man! Someone will see you!"

"Next Thursday!"

"Yeah — *if* everything goes right. Because nothing seems to be happening diplomatically, and the za'im is getting antsy. So we'll plan for next Thursday. But we've got to know that our clues are good enough, and we'll have to have our equipment and food ready, and Steven will have to have finished the reflector. If everything's *not* go, we'll wait another week." He looked around at them, and for the first time Matt saw fear in his face. "Because — it has to be perfect. If we don't do it right the first time, there sure won't be a second chance."

Thirteen

So then." Martin Vereen leaned across his conference table toward the earnest young man whose hands, emerging from immaculate French cuffs, played continuously with a paper clip. "The President must understand that I don't mean to interfere with the official efforts. He knows I wasn't happy issuing that first statement about never negotiating with terrorists; but he asked me to do it, and I did, and it's okay. But now I must act on my own, too."

The young man nodded, and a perfect fingernail slid along the paper clip. "He does understand, Senator. He's sure of your loyalty, and deeply sorry about your personal anguish. He just has reservations about what you're proposing, and wanted us to discuss them. And he wanted Kubacki to be here, since whatever you say will need to be cleared through State." They glanced at the third man present, a rangy figure with rough-cut gray hair.

Martin smiled wryly. "Kubacki hasn't had a day free of me since they set up the task force. He must think I'm his shadow."

Mike Kubacki's eyes kept their seriousness. "Hell, man. Your own *kids*. I just always wish I had more to tell you."

"My point is this. Our trial balloon about not negotiating

151

has netted us no response. So now I propose to make my own overture — completely independent, unofficial, nothing that commits the President to anything. But something that just might produce a response from Tawbah that we can use to our advantage. If it fails, the President won't have lost anything."

The White House aide frowned at Martin over his glasses. "You want to talk to them yourself."

"No. At least — not yet. I'll simply make my own formal response to their statements. Mine will take theirs at face value — assume that lessening the nuclear danger *is* their chief aim, and reiterate what my record has always shown: that I support every sensible measure that will help put brakes on the arms race.

"I'll speak to the issue of responsibility. I'll agree, not that the U.S. is guilty of anything, but that it does indeed have a heavy responsibility to help lead the way back from the nuclear brink. Anything wrong so far, gentlemen?"

Kubacki shrugged: negative. The paper clip tipped upward to show that the White House, too, saw no reason to object as yet.

"I will say that while I don't approve of negotiating with terrorists — I'd better add that, for consistency — I'm eager to meet with any group that cares as much about this grave U.S. responsibility as I do, and that once the six children are returned unharmed I'll meet with Tawbah at any place, at any time, to discuss it. I'll also seek continuing coverage in the American press for their views, and support in the Senate any suggestions for U.S. action which they convince me are constructive, appropriate, and practical."

The paper clip was still for some time. "That puts you way out on a lonely limb, doesn't it, Senator?"

"No. It just makes me say a little louder what I've been

saying all along. Let me tell you something. Frankly, besides being worried sick about the kids, I'm hopping mad at watching the arms-control initiative be grabbed up by this group, whoever the hell they are. The mileage these guys are getting in the world press bugs the devil out of me. Why are we sitting here waiting for people like this to kick our butt about not taking moral leadership? Let's go ahead and take it!" He hadn't meant to get into that. "Back to the issue. The new statement might get something started, without costing the President anything."

Kubacki shifted in his chair. "Well, it seems to me you're taking a political risk, but it's an intriguing one. *I* have no objection to the statement as you describe it."

The White House aide put down the paper clip. "I think the President will agree to let it go. Provided, of course, that you let us okay the actual wording."

"Of course. I'll get a draft to you both by this evening."

"Good." The younger man stood. "Thank you, Senator, for your time. Thanks to you, too, Mike. You heading back?"

"Ah, Mike." Martin gestured to delay him. "While you're here — a ten-minute update."

"Sure, though there isn't much to tell."

When they were alone, Martin sighed. "Still nothing on where the kids might be? That's incredible. How can it be, considering the vast intelligence network helping us?"

"Three words, Senator. We're convinced this group is small, organized, and disciplined. *Small* may be the most important word. The fewer people in on it, the less chance of a leak."

"Of course. Anything new happening, at all?"

"Well, one thing — we now have a really strong radio-monitoring network throughout the Middle East."

"Find anything?"

"Several things worth checking."

"For instance?"

"For instance — a receiver off the coast of Egypt has twice picked up transmissions in coded Arabic. Only twice, and too little copy to do much with — but well worth watching for."

"From Egypt?"

"Could be. Or Saudi Arabia. Or Libya. Can't say yet."

Martin rubbed his jaw. "Libya. Wouldn't that be strange?"

Kubacki looked down at his hands. "Yeah. It's one of the scenarios *I* work at, as a matter of fact."

"What do you hear from Khadafy?"

"Officially, very little — but I think he's interested. If the kids were hidden in his country, I think he'd really like to know about it."

Martin looked at him hard. "What do you mean?"

"You know what kind of maverick the guy is, Senator. From most governments, everywhere, I'd expect a quick turnover of the kids, if they got hold of them. From him, I'm not sure."

"Mike, sure, he's a maverick who makes anti-American noises. But he must have his own brand of decency, and these are *children*."

"Look, the Libyan-desert scenario is just one of the current top ten. Nothing to get excited about." He stood up and for a moment turned full face to Martin. "Senator, I pray for the big break in this, every day. Hang in."

"Thanks. Meanwhile, let's try to make them talk to us some more. I'll get a draft over to you quickly. I hope you get back there now without being mobbed by the press."

Kubacki shook his head. "Oh, they're getting bored with me. I never have that big story. But after you release your statement, Senator, they'll never leave you alone."

Fourteen

Now that there was a specific goal at last, the days seemed to move more quickly. Sidney steadily picked up new distinctions in dialect. Walking and working with their guards, all the boys watched for anything that could be a clue. Behind the curtain, Jessica worked on her topographical drawing. In the evenings she brought it out so the boys could sketch the area to the south; and Sidney drew an arrow indicating the direction to the town of Beerte.

But often, resting back against the wall to watch the others through half-shut eyes, Matt would admit to himself that he was increasingly afraid of disaster. What if the guards noticed that Gib and Sidney did not come back from the latrine, and chased them at once? They would surely be caught. What would happen then? Or what if the six of them had miscalculated distance or direction, and Gib and Sidney did get away only to die from exposure on some remote mountain or desert? Or from being attacked by strangers? And meanwhile — how much worse would things be for the four who were left?

He was almost relieved that some of the escape projects hit snags. The boys found no chance to get hold of a second water bag. Martha announced grumpily that she must have

155

missed one of the plane's flights; she had plotted two trips north per week, but only one trip south. Worst of all, Steven's crew mates had been working so near him that he could not risk building the reflector. Using a flat-sided stone as Gib had coached him, he had managed to pry three hubcaps loose from the old car; but he had had to hide them in a tiny cave partway up the cliff until he could finish the job without the risk of being seen.

Wednesday night Gib made it official: they would have to postpone the escape. They sat sprawled against the walls, glowering at each other. "We just can't do it. Once they discover we're gone, they're going to lock the rest of you up for good. Before that happens, we've got to have the reflector in place to bull's-eye this spot from the air."

Jessica sighed. "*Next* Thursday, then." She turned away and pulled a strand of hair across her face. She was afraid, too, Matt realized; she wasn't any surer than he that the escape plan was right. Was there anything else she was hiding, when she hid her face like that? But Gib was also watching her — and Matt dropped his own eyes.

Sidney stretched out flat on the floor and moaned. "Steve, what day is tomorrow?"

"Thursday."

"I know that, dummy. What *date?*"

"Um — September third."

"So *next* Thursday will be September tenth. Hey!" He sat up abruptly. "We'll reach the coast on September twelfth, my bar mitzvah day! How do you like that? No bar mitzvah, after all, but a freedom day." He lay down again and folded his arms across his chest. "I guess, if I have to, I can wait for that."

Gib said that he and Sidney should have some sort of rope along, in case of emergencies, and something better to carry food in; so Friday was spent getting these things ready to add to the small pile of escape equipment hidden behind the curtain. Jessica sat against the wall, fashioning two food sacks out of old T-shirts. Gib and Matt tore some of the other old clothes into long strips, which they braided tightly into a short rope. "It's pretty weird-looking," Gib decided, testing it, "but it'll hold a lot of weight, if it has to. It's frustrating to wait this whole other week, but we'll be glad we did. It pays to take time to do things right."

"I don't know, Gib," Matt said. "This whole idea still scares the shoes off me."

Gib kept on checking knots. "The alternative is lousy," he said. "We can't back off *now.*"

On Saturday, when the boys arrived back from the wadi, Steven's eyes were shiny with excitement. As soon as it was safe, he told his story. "It's set up, and it's perfect! I did it both ways, like you said, Gib — two hubcaps upside down, to focus the sun real sharp, and one right side up, to spread it wider."

"You're absolutely positive that no one saw you?" Jessica's fingers pulled nervously at the skin of her throat.

"Yup. Bakhit told me to go farther up today to look for new stone places. I never saw anybody at all from lunchtime on."

"You fit them in tight, and you're sure they don't show from below?" Gib's voice trembled with excitement. "And you aimed 'em eastward and upward, like we said?"

"Yup." Steven's smile of pride was out of control.

"Way to go!" gasped Sidney. "Man, look at my goose pimples! Freedom, here we come."

"Forget goose pimples," retorted Gib. "Concentrate on clues. And practice thinking in Italian." He looked around at the others. "Just one more thing. We gotta get another water bag."

But during the next two days, no one could. "Do you *have* to have two?" asked Martha Monday night, when Gib was glum with worry.

"Well, we'll go even if we only have one — but that would really be dangerous. We don't know how fast we'll dehydrate, traveling hard in the heat. So, everyone, keep trying. And for gosh sakes, don't get caught doing it!"

On Tuesday Matt, placing rocks all morning, knelt very near one of his crew's water bags. But several of the crew came often to squat there and tip it up for drinks; it would be quickly missed. He would have to hope for better luck at lunch.

However, at the end of lunch, the two bags that had been passed around were casually carried off by guards. Matt watched them go, and cursed inwardly.

At a late afternoon break he saw his first chance. When the crew got up to stretch and return to work, an empty bag was left in the shade near where he was sitting. Adrenaline surged through him.

No one seemed to be watching. He stood up, moved sideways, then sat down again, to retie the rags around his hands. When he stood up once more, the water bag was hidden inside his clothing. His heart pounded wildly as he hurried back to his place at the dike. Only after he had placed a dozen rocks without hearing a shout or feeling a tap on his shoulder could he dare to believe he might get away with it. He wiped sweat out of his eyes with a trembling arm, took a deep breath, and reached for another rock.

But Abou was a careful manager. When work was over and he had made his count of the tools, he pointed at the two remaining water bags and called out to the crew in an annoyed tone. Breathless with fear, Matt joined in a search of the area. Finally Abou shrugged and ordered them back toward home. But his face was clouded, and as they climbed

158

up away from the wadi he stopped twice to look back. Matt's secret burden grew heavier with each step.

That night at supper they began hiding food to save for the journey. Matt waited till Mustapha had left with the washed dishes before he pulled out his prize. Even while the others swarmed over him in excitement, he was thinking: Abou did not yet seem to suspect the theft. But after the escape — wouldn't he finally make the connection? And wouldn't that destroy their carefully fabricated explanation of Gib's and Sidney's disappearance? What would happen then?

When Assad had looked in at them and the door had been barred for the night, Gib whispered into the dark, "We're go. Forty-eight hours to liftoff, and counting." Shivering, Matt wrapped himself more tightly in his blanket.

The next morning the wind wheeled once more and began to blow from the desert — steady, hot, laden with dust. Work at the wadi went slowly and ended early. To Matt's relief, Abou seemed to make no reference to the water bag. After supper Matt and Steven watched at the windows while Sidney rehearsed his dialect clues with Martha as audience, and Jessica brought out the escape supplies for Gib's final inspection: the two sacks fattening with bread, cheese, and dates; the water bags, just now filled with fresh water; the homemade rope; and two crude tool-weapons — sharp-edged pieces of metal Steven had smuggled in from the old car.

"Hey," protested Jessica. "That thing's rusty. You might get tetanus if you cut yourself with that."

Gib made a face back at her. "The idea is to give tetanus to anything that tries to mess with us."

She turned away from him abruptly, went to the long wall, and put out a finger to touch Adam's hand. From his post at the window Matt could see only the side of her face. Gib sat looking after her. "Hey, Jess," he said after a minute. "Joke."

She shook her head. "*No* joke, what you two are doing. I don't like it when you make it sound like some fabulous adventure." But soon she turned back to watch what he was doing.

Sidney finished a catalogue of words. "That's all of them."

Martha shook her head. "Nope — you forgot one."

"I did not. What do *you* know about it?"

"You forgot *gabilah.*"

"Oh, yeah. Fuad says *gabilah,* but the others —"

Assad's approach was quiet and quick. Matt, on guard at the front window, did not turn to see him till he was nearly to the door. Then he whispered a warning that sent everyone else scrambling to hide the escape supplies behind the curtain, while he himself lounged back against the window, trying to block Assad's gaze with his body. Assad strode into the room, already talking.

"I am called to go to meet with the za'im and the council of advisors, to discuss your future! This will be a very important meeting. But Fuad says bad weather is coming, so I must leave at once to avoid it. I will be away several days. You will obey Fuad in all things." He stepped forward, frowning. "What is *that?*"

Matt followed his gaze, and froze. Assad was staring at one end of the crude escape rope, trailing out from behind the curtain.

For a moment no one moved. Then Jessica ran to the rope, stooped. "Oh, we'll show you, Assad. It's a jump rope, a game. All American girls love it. Show him, Martha, quickly."

Martha caught the rope and went into action. The rope tapped the low ceiling, and her short, flaxen hair bounced.

160

"Let's see now. Here goes, 'Teddy bear, teddy bear, turn around —' "

"Ide-hay the awter-way," said Jessica clearly.

"I go to the za'im. I do not have the time —"

"Just a second, Assad! Watch her. Watch what comes next." Martha's teddy bear was touching the ground between jumps. Now Jessica stared at Gib. *"Ide-hay the awter-way!"*

Assad looked from Martha to Jessica, frowning. "What? What is it you say?"

"It's the name of what she's doing now. Watch!"

Understanding at last, Matt looked wildly around the room. Both stolen water bags, fat and waiting, rested against the wall near Gib. Assad would see them the minute he turned. Matt gestured frantically. Gib frowned at him, turned, saw the bags — and crouched at once between them, hiding them with his robe.

In the next second Assad had reached for the rope, and swung around. "Such a thing you may not have. You will make no toys unless you first discuss with me. We will speak more of this when I return."

The quiet after he left was profound. Nauseated and shaking, Matt slid down the wall till he was sitting on the floor. The room seemed to pulsate, enlarging and contracting before his eyes. The only sound was Jessica's quick step as she rescued the bags from Gib and hid them once again behind the curtain. Then she sank to the floor and hid her face in her hands.

"Good job, Jess," said Gib, his own tipped-up face white. "Super, super job. You too, Marth. Sorry. We shouldn't have had all the stuff in here at once."

Matt shut his eyes to stop the room from moving. "I should have seen him coming sooner. Much, much sooner."

They sat in silence for a long time, reeling from the close call.

Sidney exhaled a long, slow breath. "Well, as soon as I can move, I'm going to bed. Tomorrow is a big one."

"Hey, he said bad weather's coming," Matt remembered. "What do you suppose that means? What if it makes trouble for you, Gib?"

"Nothing can stop us now. Do you realize? Assad's being away is perfect! Without him, they won't know what to do when they *do* find us gone! Sidney's right — we'd better sleep. Some of us won't get any, *tomorrow* night."

They were all on their mats before the sky was dark. "Jessica," asked Steven, just loudly enough that she could hear him through the curtain, "was that really supposed to be a jump rope?"

Matt glared at Sidney to keep him from laughing, but Sidney wasn't laughing. "No," Jessica answered. "I made that up. It's really a you-know-what rope."

"But I'll tell you something," said Gib, his voice sounding thick. "When we get home, we'll make another one just like it to show everybody, and they'll put it up on a huge plaque in the Smithsonian with a title in big gold letters: JESSICA'S JUMP ROPE."

"Mine, too," said Martha, in a reasonable tone.

"Yes," said Matt. "Martha's, too."

For all of them the night was long and restless. The steady hot wind set up a dull howling in the rocks, which alone would have made a good sleep unlikely; the approaching adventure made it impossible. Matt and Gib had been awake and whispering for some time when, just after the guards' daybreak prayers, Fuad unbarred the door. "Everyone wake now. Eat.

I come for talk very soon." Startled, they woke the others. When Mustapha brought breakfast he shook his head in warning, pointed south, and drew a corner of his kaffiyeh across his face.

They were waiting for Fuad when he returned, carrying a piece of heavy black goat-hair tenting. "Not work at wadi now. *Ghibli* coming. Red wind, bad wind. Much sand. Stay inside. Woman go for water now, quick. Man and Fuad work windows."

Jessica and Martha left at a jog, their clothes snapping in the wind. Their guard carried several water bags hung from his shoulders. Gesturing to the boys to watch, Fuad cut three large rectangles from the piece of tenting and folded them in half. Next he demonstrated how each of these was to have its edges strengthened by extra folds, through which spikes would be driven into the outside wall of the hut, until a double layer of heavy cloth covered each window like a shutter. He helped with the first shutter, showing how tight the cloth should be pulled and how close together the nails should be placed. Then he left them and hurried to begin the same task on the other hut.

"Lord," Gib muttered. "A real hammer in my hand again! Don't I wish I could go off with this!"

Matt pulled the cloth taut. "I don't think you should go. Look how much dust is in the air already. Look, Gib, look across the ravine." A reddish haze of dust was beginning to obscure the opposite wall of rock.

Gib turned back to his work. "We might never get another chance. Come on, tighter."

Soon the daylight began to wane to a lurid red glow. They squinted and coughed from the dust in the air. "Steven," said Gib suddenly, "go inside. You shouldn't be breathing this stuff." Steven obeyed without a word.

The girls returned as they were finishing. "Look at the water," said Jessica, peering into her pail. "It's opaque with sand already."

"It'll settle," said Gib. "Let's get inside." They followed him, stumbling against each other in the near-dark interior.

Fuad and Mustapha arrived to collect the tools and deliver a big bowl of cold mashed chickpeas and a basket of bread. "For many times eat," Fuad explained. "Your water only for drink. Not wash. Maybe you must sit inside house much time."

"What about going to the latrine?" asked Steven.

"Go to latrine now. Quick. Very soon we lock door. After lock door" — he gestured to an old gallon oil can he had set inside the room — "*that* is latrine."

Someone called, and he left at a run. "Boy," said Matt. "How do you suppose they're getting ready for this down in the tents?"

Gib's urgency drowned him out. "Quick, everybody! They've closed down the guard post. Sid and I have gotta get out of here *now* — fast, before Fuad gets back. Jess, get the stuff."

"Now?" asked Martha, her voice high. "The storm's starting!"

"You heard him — any minute they're going to bar the door, maybe for days. It's go now, or not till the storm's over, and that'll be too late. Matt, give me the sandals. *Hurry up!*"

Matt pulled them off, fighting himself. "No! Don't go! The storm's sure to be bad, or Fuad wouldn't be making such a fuss."

"But it guarantees us even more time, don't you see? From now all the way till Saturday morning. About forty-five hours. And no Assad to take charge! Damn this thing." He finally stamped the sandal into place. "Martha, quick, get Jess's map

164

of the area. The rest of the clues are in our heads. What have I forgotten?"

"Gib!" Jessica's voice was fierce. "Don't go! Wait till next week. The storm could kill you."

"So could next week," said Gib, handing Sidney one of the homemade tools and tying the other into his own belt. "Who· knows what the za'im is going to tell Assad? Hurry up — the water bags."

"For God's sake, no!" cried Matt. "You don't know anything about sandstorms."

"Don't listen to 'em, Gib!" cried Sidney, fastening the loop of his water bag. "It's our only chance. For everyone."

"When it gets bad we can hide in a cave." Gib grabbed up the food bags and opened the door a crack. A rush of sand swirled through it. "Here we go. Good-bye, everyone. Next guests — the Marines. Jess, you and Martha play your parts now, *quick!*"

They slammed the door shut behind them.

Frozen, the others listened for sounds of interception, but there were none — only the growing howl of the wind, blurred by the soft whirl of sand against the blank south wall of the hut. Then Jessica and Martha jumped to roll out Gib's and Sidney's mats and curled up on them in the boys' blankets.

"Steven, you okay?" Matt peered at the child. Steven nodded. He was pale and wide-eyed, but his breathing seemed normal. "You and I'd better lie down, too." Matt grabbed for his own mat. "The storm scares us and we're trying to sleep. Jess, lie out straight; you still look like a girl. That's better."

Without warning, there was a noise outside the door. Again there was a violent assault of sand as someone with his kaffiyeh across his face — Sadik? — peered in, then pulled the door shut once more and shoved the bar into place.

Slowly they emerged from their blankets, sat up. With every second, the howl of the wind grew louder — a terrifying, unrelenting crescendo. "Pretty impressive sound effects," said Matt, speaking to make a calm, human noise, just as Gib would have done at this moment.

No one answered him. Through the gloom they watched the start of the invasion of sand — through the cracks of the door, in under the edges of the goatskin shutters, driven by a frantic force that dissipated quickly inside the closed room and dropped its cargo in yellow wisps.

Steven coughed. Jessica looked at him, then around the room. "Let's cover the water and food. Stevie, maybe you should lie down again. I'll wet your kaffiyeh and put it over you, and you'll have your own private tent."

"Oh, not over my eyes," said Steven. "And I want to sit up, with you guys. I think I'll be all right."

Jessica draped the wet cloth across his nose and tied it behind his head. "Good. Now you look like an Arab-American bandit. And you can lift the bottom for more air whenever you need to." She had to speak loudly, over the storm.

Then there was nothing more to do. Matt watched the sand and thought with terror of the two outside. How could they survive this? He did not dare to meet Jessica's eyes. Martha and Steven sat wrapped in their blankets, hunched and still.

"The Lord is my shepherd," Jessica began finally, her voice trembling. "I shall not want . . ."

The hours were interminable. They ate little. After what seemed a lifetime, judging that finally the dark had come — the real dark of night — they tried to sleep.

Sometime later Matt was startled awake by Jessica's shaking him. "Listen!"

166

Over the steady howl of the wind, he could hear a scratching at the door. "Somebody's trying to open it! Oh, God." Together they scrambled to the door, but there was nothing they could do except wait. The younger two woke at the noise and sat watching. Steven's mask looked like a great white beak.

Finally the bar slid free and the door flew open. It was Sidney, choking and alone. They pulled him into the room, where he collapsed. "Get Gib. Down there. Below the latrine."

Dawn was penetrating the laden air enough to light it faintly with the same unearthly red, but they could see no farther than a few yards. Shielding their faces with their kaffiyehs, Jessica and Matt plunged into the storm. They worked as a team — she not leaving sight of the hut till he signaled that he had located a remembered hump of rock on the way to the latrine, then she following to stay at that point till he had reached another landmark. Soon after they started down into the ravine Matt heard a faint call: "Here, here." Gib was lying under an overhang of rock with his robe over his head.

Matt had to cough out sand before he could shout to him. "Are you hurt?"

"My foot. Exhausted."

"Here we go." Leaning into the rock, Jessica and Matt shoved and pulled him up till they had reached the top of the ravine. Then Jessica scouted the way, returning to help with Gib only when she had sighted the next landmark. Pulling Gib's arm tight across his shoulders, Matt half-carried his brother home.

Home is what it almost felt like when they were safely inside again, with the door shut against the wind. They laid Gib down on the ground and collapsed, coughing and gasping. Martha and Steven brought cups of water to rinse out their mouths and a damp rag for their faces. Finally they wet the rag once more and tucked it around Gib's swollen, purple foot.

It seemed like a long time before Sidney had recovered enough to explain. "We got through the fissure and started out on the level land. But it got too bad. We couldn't see. We could hardly even breathe. So we went back into the fissure to wait it out. But the sand came roaring in, even there. Pouring down. Oh, wow, I thought it would drown us. So we gave up and pushed the food and stuff into a big crack. Except the map; we've got the map. Here, Jess, you'd better hide it again.

"Then we tried to climb back. It was murder, trying to hold onto the rocks in all that sand. Gib slipped off and fell, about ten feet down. Then I thought we were really going to die. But he climbed back and we kept coming. He said he'd keep on till we could see the latrine, and he did. We waited there till dawn. Then I came on, but I couldn't find the hut! It seemed to be hours."

Pain sat in Matt's chest like a rock. "Gib, man. You gonna be okay?"

"Maybe. Someday." His eyes were closed, and the white face was frighteningly taut.

"Your foot hurts that bad?"

"My foot and my soul, man. Goddamn fool. Goddamn fool." Tears slid out of his eyes and down his face. Matt put his own face into his hands to hide from the sight.

The storm lasted through Friday and Friday night. Saturday morning they woke to astonishing silence; the wind was still. When Fuad came to the hut early, he was upset to find the door unbarred. Gib explained that before the storm he had been the last to go to the latrine, and had fallen on the rocks. "You guys locked me out," he said, indignantly. "Good thing I could drag myself back and get that door open."

Fuad frowned in confusion. "But Sadik say, you here!"

Gib paused but did not falter. "Well, of course it was dark as *night* in here. Too bad for me he thought he saw me. I sure could have used some *help*, lying out there on the rocks!"

Fuad examined Gib's foot and said that a little time would heal it, if Allah willed.

Fifteen

As it happened, the ordeal of the sand was not yet fully over; but, for the first bright hours of Saturday, it seemed to be.

When Fuad had looked at Gib's foot, he released the other hostages to unshutter the windows, go for water, and brush the sand out of the hut. The morning was cool and crystalline, and the fresh breeze from the north was so benign that Matt found the two days of the storm almost more amazing in memory than they had been in fact. The bleak landscape itself seemed little changed; most of the sand had blown on to settle in lower places.

Once the entire camp had been tidied, Fuad ordered the work crews out to the wadi for the afternoon, to check out the effects of the storm. They left Gib behind with the girls, his eyes dulled with discouragement.

Sidney, too, was in the depths of gloom. He muttered to Matt as they walked toward the wadi. "I can't believe this. Today was to be my bar mitzvah. Then it was to be the day Gib and I reached the coast, free. Instead, here I am, back on the chain gang, doing the same damn thing as three days ago. How in the world are we ever going to get home now?"

Some distance ahead, the solemn young Sadik turned to

look back. Seeing Sidney, he raised his hand high in greeting.

"Good," said Matt. "That looks friendly enough. I sure hope Sadik thinks it was his eyes and not *us* that pulled that trick on him. Since now you've got to go on working with him."

"Man, what a bummer," groaned Sidney. "He's the only half-decent thing about building dikes. If he ever figured out I put one over on him, that would really louse things up."

As they reached the lower areas, they could see increasing evidence of the storm. Along the valley of the wadi, its results were awesome. The wadi itself was little affected, but the rock walls on either side looked vastly different. Wherever a cliff face had blocked the wind, a drift of sand had grown in the corresponding lee. Some of these drifts were huge and hid the familiar hillsides. Several piles of rocks waiting at the foot of the cliffs were completely hidden; in other places, the slopes used as chutes for sliding rocks down to the valley floor had been made useless by the new aprons of sand.

Matt's crew set to work clearing a new chute. Farther along the valley, Steven's and Sidney's crew searched for buried rock piles. After a while the young Sadik began digging determinedly into the base of a large drift that Matt could see, from his angle, had a strangely high and varied crestline. At the time, he thought only how beautiful the drift was, as the irregular crest sent the afternoon shadows left here, right there.

Suddenly there was a shout — Sidney's voice — and then a soft but voluminous sliding noise. Shading his eyes to look, Matt could see only a growing cloud of dust — rising from the spot where Sadik had been working.

Now shouting himself, Matt began to run toward the sandslide. Behind him came the rest of his own crew, but where in hell were all the others? Ahead of him he could see no one at all. Then, as the cloud of dust began to clear, he saw Sidney — Sidney digging frantically into the sand, bellowing· in English, digging still, reaching something, pulling, falling backward, digging and pulling again. He had hold of an arm, and as the sand slid and shifted and slid further, tumbling him again and again, he held onto it, until at last the others reached him, Matt himself reached him, and five or six of them together were finally able to pull Sadik's limp body out of the sand. He was not breathing.

And then there seemed to be no one but Sidney and Matt, themselves tortured for air, who knew the magic that might restore breath — spilling sand out of Sadik's mouth, tipping his head back, pinching his nose shut, blowing into his mouth, again and again.

They took turns, changing every few seconds because they had to. Matt noticed with a distant interest that the whole world seemed to have turned blue. They worked and worked. The guards watched. No one spoke. After a tiny eternity, Sadik's body shuddered with its own intake of air, and he was breathing.

Poor Sidney, Matt thought, when the world had returned to its normal colors and his head had begun to clear. For the second time in two days, the younger boy lay on the ground, exhausted. When he finally opened his eyes he was looking up at a circle of respectful Arab faces. "Oh, God," he groaned, closing them again. "No more sand. Please, never any more sand."

That evening Gib and the girls made them tell the whole story several times. Mustapha returned after supper with a special treat of oranges and tea-with-peanuts. Finally Fuad came to offer Sidney and Matt his grave appreciation. When he left he handed Sidney a gift from Sadik: a chubby, stylized little silver hand on a narrow thong. "Fatima," he explained, frowning a little. "Is maybe not good Islam. But is Sadik's wish."

"Does that mean Sadik is trying to convert you?" asked Martha, when Fuad had gone.

"Of course not," said Jessica. "He's wishing Sidney good luck. He's saying thanks. That's nice."

Martha watched as Sidney slipped the thong over his head, then doubled his chin in order to look down at the little hand. "Sidney, do you like Sadik?" she asked.

"Of course not." He glared at her. "Don't be so dumb. He's a terrorist Arab kidnaper. How could I like him?"

"Then how come you worked so hard to save his life?"

He played with the little hand and was silent for some time. Finally he shrugged. "I don't know. Sadik and I — we moved a lot of stones together."

Sidney's quiet mood spread a strange but comfortable silence among them all. Matt, trying not to look at Gib's misshapen foot, winced for him when he tried to move it.

Suddenly Sidney leaned forward. "Has the sun set yet?"

"No." Jessica looked out the window. "It must be nearly down, but the guards aren't gathering yet for prayers."

"Good." He got up. "Then it's still my Sabbath." He looked around the room. "Rats. Not even a handkerchief?"

"What do you want?" Jessica asked.

From a corner, Sidney grabbed up the remains of his old jeans; with several hefty tugs he ripped off a back pocket. "A yarmulke." He set the small patch of cloth on the top of his head. "There. Gotta have a yarmulke."

He went to the front window and looked out for a moment, making a strange sight for the rest of them: a slight figure in an Arab robe, whose straight dark hair in a grown-out American haircut was topped by a patch of faded denim. The new charm swung as he turned, and he caught it in his fist to steady it.

"This is my first bar mitzvah. Later on, you're all invited to my other one. *This* one'll just take a second." Through the window, a pale flush still lighted the sky.

"The words I am going to say are the holiest words in the Torah. They're simple, but they're mysterious, too. Only, today I think they got clearer for me."

He looked around at his congregation and cleared his throat. The hand beneath his chin still clutched Sadik's gift.

"*'Shema yisrael Adonai Eloheinu Adonai ehad.'*

"Hear, O Israel: the Lord our God, the Lord is One."

Sixteen

Sunday dawned as a day without hope. They had little to say to each other as they returned to their hostage routine. For Matt, the hardest part was coming back from work at the wadi to sit looking at the desolation in Gib's eyes.

Only Steven and Sidney resisted the tide of despair. "Why can't we go ahead with the plan?" Sidney protested at dinner. "The only difference is, somebody else goes with me. It's still a good idea. Matt, come on, man. You come with me."

Matt shook his head. "I think we should stay together now. Besides, we've blown our getaway. We could never fool them again by disguising the girls in blankets."

Martha gazed glumly into her tea. "What *do* we do, then?"

"We wait and watch," Gib said finally, in a flat voice. "We've used our brains this far, and we just keep doing it."

"Maybe when Assad gets back there'll be something new from the za'im," said Jessica. "You know, negotiations or something." But she looked away after she'd spoken, and no one answered her.

"Here he comes now!" announced Steven, after a little while.

"What?"

"Here comes Assad! I hear the truck."

Matt ran to the window with the others; but it was a long time before Assad arrived at the hut, examined Gib's foot in silence, then sat down and frowned at them. "You are in very much trouble. Your government still makes no response. Your father" — he glanced at Matt — "makes one little noise. That is *all*."

Matt's heart leapt. "What did Dad say?"

"Why should I tell you? It is a very little thing he says; it is not important. Except" — his expression grew more subtle — "I, Assad, have used it to win for you a chance to go home."

Gib picked up the cue. "What do you mean?"

Assad tipped his head back dramatically. "Some of the council say it is time to take the next step, to show the U.S. that we will increase the pressure until they agree to our demands." He peered at them threateningly from beneath lowered lids. "But I said, 'Wait, my brothers. This senator has just made one small gesture to us. He is an important man, and he is not so evil as some Americans. Look — he has already spoken out for a nuclear freeze.' "

Now he looked sideways at Matt. "I showed them the article from the newspaper, with the picture of you and your father. I said, 'And see, it was this man's son who persuaded him to do this thing. We have this son as a hostage. I will tell this son to write to the senator, in his own writing, telling him to agree to our demands, and to get his powerful friends to agree, too.' "

Suddenly Matt was shaking with rage. Damn him, he thought. He can kill me if he wants to. "I'll never do that."

"You will!" Assad's own voice rose in anger. But there was something else in his face — something tense and precarious.

"I will not."

Assad jumped to his feet, but Gib stretched a hand toward him. "Assad! Don't listen to my brother now. He's still upset by the storm. Let me talk to him tonight. Please come back in the morning, when his head is clear. Maybe you could bring a copy of the demands, so he'll know exactly what they are."

Assad's nostrils flared, but he kept his gaze on Gib. "I will come back in the morning," he said finally. "I will bring the statement." He clashed the bar shut behind him, angrily.

Gib waved Martha and Sidney to the windows and turned to Matt. "You idiot. You may have ruined our last chance to get home."

"Shut up, Gib," said Jessica. "Matt, listen! We might really get some leverage out of this."

Matt was still flaming. "That bastard comes in here hinting that Dad's made a statement, then he won't tell us what; he just says I'm going to write a note home saying, 'Please, Dad, do everything these nice people want.' Well, bullshit to that."

Jessica's hand was out, insistently shushing Gib. "Matt, please, listen. For the first time, Assad *needs* us. Or, he needs *you*. Didn't you see? He was scared, there at the end! He's convinced those guys to let him try to pull this thing off. Do you think he wants to go back and say, 'Sorry, fellahs, stupid me, I goofed'?"

Gib stretched out his own hand to lower Jessica's, but he was cooler now. "That's the point, Matt. For the first time since we were kidnaped we're in a position to negotiate. You're the one who's supposed to be so hot on negotiating!"

"Well, I'm sure as hell not going to do what he said."

"Of course not. But look, he really believes you can influence Dad. There's got to be a way to capitalize on that. We have all night to figure out how to do it. Let's get going."

There was silence for a little while, but it began to feel

177

like the lively simmer of conspiracy. "We're not going to like their statement," Jessica began tentatively. "But — suppose we drafted our own. It'd have to have the stuff they want to hear, but it could have a lot of our own stuff, too — what we really believe. Things that some people in Congress could even agree with."

Gib picked it up. "So we could argue that it might get some real support — *if* we could get Dad behind it. Aha — now it's coming. And the way to get Dad behind it is to send *Matt* to sell it to him."

"Send me *home?*" Matt felt the blood drain from his face. Then he shook his head. "Look, there's no way I'm going home to try to argue Dad into anything. That's baloney."

"Of course not, you jerk." Gib whispered it, hoarsely. "That's just what we *say*. Don't you see? You're going home to deliver the clues!"

When Assad arrived promptly after breakfast, they were ready for him. "Morning, Assad," said Matt, seriously. "I'm sorry about last night."

Assad ignored him and addressed Gib. "Here is the statement."

"Thanks," said Gib. "Can I read it aloud?" Assad gave the downward half of a nod. Gib leaned back against the wall and began.

"Tawbah, a pan-Islamic brotherhood, has taken hostage the children of American legislators to force the United States to face its responsibility for the nuclear disaster now threatening the world . . ."

Outside, the work crews were leaving for the wadi without them.

"That is a fine statement," said Assad, when Gib had finished. He pounded the ground. "It tells only the truth. It is a good start for negotiating. Yet it has no response!"

"The problem isn't the wording," said Sidney. "The problem is that you expect the U.S. to negotiate when you've kidnaped —" He stopped abruptly under Gib's steely glare.

"Wrong, Sidney," said Gib firmly. "The problem *is* how the statement sounds —"

But Assad gestured angrily at Sidney. "That is stupid! A country negotiates *only* under pressure. If Tawbah did not have American hostages, would anyone publish, even *read* our demands? No. Yet now the whole world speaks of this document and its justice. We are most pleased. Yet — no response."

It was time Matt got into this. Carefully. "You've lived in the States, Assad. You know how we think about ourselves. We couldn't respond to a statement that makes us sound so evil."

Gib was nodding. "Americans are proud and stubborn. We can't negotiate if we have to start from other people's angry accusations about us."

Matt went on. "Assad, if I wrote to my father asking him to agree to your demands, there's no way he'd do it. He'd even think you must have forced me to write that. But if I write a statement myself — if together the six of us write one, something that says the same thing yours does, but in our own way — that will be different. *Of course* he'll respond to that. We'll write this for you because it'll help you get what you want, so we can go home."

Assad frowned at Matt. "You think your father would respond?"

"Actually, there's only one way to be sure." Gib's voice was amazingly steady. "When the statement is ready, and Tawbah is satisfied with it, it should be personally delivered to our father by Matt. You're right, Assad, that Matt is one of Dad's most trusted advisers. If he's there to defend it — that's your best chance of getting Dad's support."

It was preposterous. Was Assad going to buy it? Matt did not dare glance at his face.

"Besides," said Jessica, "Senator Vereen must be furious at Tawbah right now. He'll feel a lot more willing to listen to your ideas if you show good faith by sending one son home."

"Meanwhile," Gib went on, "think of the propaganda gold mine you'd have. Even if you still got no official U.S. response. Or even no response from Dad! You'd have a strong antinuclear statement freely composed by six children of American leaders. Man, the TV cameras of the world would eat it up, wouldn't they? And there'd be Matt, arguing for the statement on camera, insisting that we mean it."

A variety of expressions flickered across Assad's face. Shading his eyes with a hand, he took counsel with himself. Finally he looked up, at Matt. "How are we sure that when you get home you will not renounce your statement?"

Matt bristled. "It's too bad you don't know me as well as you know my father. Don't you think I have any integrity?" But that was absurd; because of course he would tell any lie in the world to get the six of them safely home.

But Gib was nodding at him approvingly. "Besides, Assad, what good would that do us? You'd still have no negotiations, so the five of us would still be sitting here. No, no, why do you think we're suggesting this? Because it's the only way of getting the U.S. response you want, so you'll let the rest of us go home."

Again Assad looked searchingly from one face to another. *We* are the foreign land *he's* lost in, thought Matt, in surprise. He doesn't know his way out, either.

Assad stood. "I will communicate with the za'im about this.

For today, you three boys will go to work as usual. Fuad worries that work is slow because of the ghibli."

They did not see Assad again until early the next morning. But when he arrived, he brought news: the za'im and the council of advisers tentatively agreed to the proposal. The Americans could proceed at once to draft a statement, which must call upon the U.S. to disarm itself completely and unilaterally of all nuclear weapons, beginning immediately. If the statement did not win the approval of Tawbah, the idea would be dropped. If the statement *were* approved, it would be smuggled to some neutral point for release — with Matt accompanying it as spokesman and symbol of good faith.

Assad, who seemed jittery, had his own instructions to add. They would start at once, this morning. Matt and Sidney would not go to the wadi. Steven, however, was too young to contribute much to the statement; he would go with his crew. Assad did not even mention Jessica and Martha. If they were going to help, he'd rather ignore the fact.

As soon as the girls had returned with water, the five of them set to work. Matt pulled the low table into the center of the room and they grouped themselves around it, with Gib — who could not sit cross-legged — stretched out, leaning on his elbow. Assad brought Matt a tablet of paper and two pencils, then sat down against the wall. "You are lucky to have this chance." He *was* nervous; he wiped sweat from his face. "The za'im is not convinced. He allows this as a favor to me. So — do a good job. I will be here to supervise you. Go ahead, start now."

Matt looked down at the blank tablet in front of him. "I guess we're about to begin the most important thinking we've ever done. The hardest part will be getting clear on the points we want to make. Let's begin by suggesting what they ought to be." He looked around the table. They had not had much time to prepare, and they had not guessed they would have to work in front of Assad. Most of the faces staring back seemed blank, a little frightened.

Sitting next to Matt, Martha hunched her shoulders and shivered. Her amazed whisper was soft; perhaps no one but Matt heard it. "Geez. I can't believe we're for real."

Seventeen

Many times during that day Matt recognized in himself the same shiver of astonishment that he had seen in Martha. Of course, what they were doing around the low table *was* desperately "for real"; they were trying to save their lives. But they could do that only by means of the most elaborate pretending: by writing a statement that must seem sincere and convincing in itself, though its real goal was simply to win the approval of Tawbah.

It was intense and difficult work. In the late afternoon Matt called a halt for the day, on account of general exhaustion. Assad left, looking a little weary himself. Alone at last, they stretched out to rest.

"Hey," said Martha, after a little while, "do you guys *believe* all this stuff we're saying?"

"Yes," said Jessica.

"No," said Sidney.

"It doesn't matter," said Gib.

But it will, thought Matt. If the statement goes home, and I go with it, it will end up mattering a lot to me.

That was the way Steven found them when he returned — stretched out and silent; but when Mustapha brought rice balls and dates, they began to recover. After supper Jessica and

Martha stood guard at the windows, while Gib and Sidney began to coach Matt on the clues. "Less than fifty miles from the coast, maybe a whole lot less. Rugged limestone mountains. I go over Jessica's drawing with them. Beerte and the mosque. The little French plane passes us to the east, flying south on Saturdays and Wednesdays about midmorning . . ."

The dialect clues were desperately hard for Matt. "Forget it, Sidney," he groaned finally. "Nobody but you can *hear* those differences, much less speak them. We'll have to rely on the other clues."

"Come on, man, it's too important. Try this one. Everybody calls Steven 'asghar.' It probably means 'the little guy' or something. But Khaled says it like this: 'asghar.' Hear that difference in the 'g' sound?"

Matt did not. From the window, Martha breathed a chuckle.

Sidney tried again. "Okay, try 'ru'aq.' That's what they call that curtain. But the locals say 'ru'aq.' Hear how that break in the middle comes from deeper in the throat? Try it, both ways."

"Ru'aq; ru'aq."

Martha was looking out the window, but Matt heard her smother a laugh in the crook of her elbow. He turned indignantly. "So what's with you? I said that just the way he did."

Martha shook her head. "No, you didn't."

"Okay, if you're such an expert, let's hear *you* say it."

"Ru'aq, and ru'aq. Asghar, and asghar."

Matt looked at Sidney, who nodded morosely. "Well, hell" — he threw up his hands in exasperation — "*I* can't hear it."

"You've *got* to," said Gib. "It's what may set us free. Shut up, Marth. Go on, Matt. Listen to Sidney say 'em again."

* * *

Late on the second afternoon they began actually drafting the statement, and Matt assured Assad that it would be ready for dispatch to the za'im by noon of the next day. That evening he sat at the side window, looking out toward the ravine, his mind skidding from the words of the statement to another silent rehearsal of the clues. The evening was cool, so cool that he had already wrapped himself in his blanket; still, sweat kept forming on his forehead.

Martha had gone to bed early. From behind the curtain he could hear an occasional moan as she turned restlessly again and again in her shallow sleep. Steven's calendar said it was five weeks since they had been abducted. How much longer could they all hold out? It seemed to him that all their hearts would break in unison if this last, incredible scheme failed. And so much of it depended on *him* . . .

But he woke in the morning unaccountably renewed, eager and wildly hopeful again. There was tense laughter during breakfast and some nervous bumping of knees under the table. "Come on, Steven," grumbled Sidney. "Haven't you learned how to sit cross-legged in that bathrobe *yet?*"

Steven frowned. "I don't bend too good when I first get up."

"*Some* people still go to work, Sidney," observed Jessica. "Have you forgotten already what it's like to wake up stiff?"

"Hurry up, Martha," said Matt. "You haven't eaten anything."

"I don't want any." Martha put down her spoon and turned away from the table. Surprised, they watched her crawl toward the window and lie down under it. "Hey," said Gib. "You just had it with mashed beans? Or are you mad about something?"

She shook her head. "My stomach feels bad."

"You want us to ask Mustapha to bring you some more tea?"

Again the headshake. "I just want to be left alone."

As soon as the breakfast cleanup was finished, Matt spread out the pages of the draft on the table. "Let's get started before Assad comes. I'll read through what we've got." He looked up at Steven, who lingered at the door.

Encouraged, the younger boy came close. "I just want to say good luck today, and I'll take care of everything outside."

It had been carefully prepared. "Thanks, man," Matt said.

Steven nodded and ran to the door. Matt turned back and picked up the first paper in front of him. "Okay, here goes."

STATEMENT OF THE SIX AMERICANS

This statement is entirely our own work and comes from our own beliefs. However, credit for its getting written belongs to Tawbah.

This statement will talk about fear, and what it can make people do. It is because fear itself has become so dangerous that we now support immediate unilateral U.S. disarmament of nuclear weapons.

Our position is based on two main ideas. We believe that:

1. If nuclear war comes, it will happen because — and only because — someone got too frightened that their enemy was about to use nuclear weapons. (So why let anyone become that afraid of *us?*)
2. Nobody needs nuclear weapons anyway, because there are no realistic uses for them, even as deterrents. In fact, as we said, more and more they risk *causing* war (through fear and miscalculation), and nations that don't have them are much safer from nuclear attack than those that do . . .

* * *

Steven broke into a run, waving ahead to Bakhit and the others to let them know he was coming, listening to the whistle of wind in his ears and the soft thudding of his bare

186

feet. Or, maybe he couldn't hear his steps, after all; maybe it was just the *feel* of them that set up a bouncing inside him, like the beginning of a song.

This was the third morning in a row he had caught the smell of the sea. The clean breeze that carried it played with him now as he ran, shoving him gently forward toward his work. The great sweep of the sky, so unlike the hot white lid that would clamp down over everything during the midday, was a pale, rinsed yellow, tinted peach at the horizon. The ridges ahead of him raised their peaks proudly into the air, and he lifted his arms to salute them. Bakhit, turning at that moment to look for him, waved back.

If people from home could see him now, he thought, they would not know him. They would see only a Beduin boy — the stern eyes, shadowed by the kaffiyeh; the strong hands, deceptively thin; the brown legs flashing beneath the robe; the bare feet toughened now to run easily over all but the most gravelly tracks and leap like a goat from rock to rock. They would think, That boy is at home in the wild desert. He probably tends animals, never sleeps under a roof, and does the work of a grown man.

They approached the last rise of their walk, beyond which the track widened and began its long slope downward. Here Bakhit often paused to wait for Steven and walk the last stretch to the wadi with him. Would he stop now? Steven caught his breath.

Sure enough, Bakhit stopped at the crest and waved his companions on. As Steven came abreast, the Arab swung carefully into stride with him. This was a game they often played — Bakhit trying to match Steven's walk, step for step; Steven trying to fool him by sudden changes of pace. This morning it was several minutes before Steven succeeded. Then they both laughed, and the game was over.

187

Bakhit patted a small cloth bag hanging from his belt. *I have something interesting here,* his hand said.

Oh? Steven let his eyes ask, *What?*

Bakhit produced an orange, which he tucked into Steven's belt. "Thank you," Steven said aloud, thinking how it would taste.

Here's something else, said Bakhit's hand. He pulled out a small, flat packet, unwrapped the cloth protection, and handed Steven a photograph glued onto cardboard. The picture was of a young Arab boy standing very straight and serious-eyed at the door of a school. He was wearing short pants, a shirt with buttons, and a cloth cap, and he was holding some books.

That's my boy, said Bakhit's hands.

How old? asked Steven's hands. *Is he as tall as I am?*

A little taller, Bakhit's hands answered. *About an inch taller.*

"I'm Steven," said Steven aloud, slapping his own chest. *What is your boy's name?* asked his finger on the picture, his raised eyebrows.

"Salem," said Bakhit aloud. *He reads many books,* Bakhit's hands went on. *He has a very good mind. And he has a bad leg. He walks with a limp.*

Steven nodded. He looked hard at the serious eyes in the picture, wondering what kinds of books Salem liked to read. Then he wondered whether Bakhit ever played the walking game with him. Oh, probably not, if the boy limped. He was suddenly glad that Bakhit's son couldn't play the game with him, and then he was ashamed of being glad. He nodded again, and touched the picture politely with a finger. "Hello, Salem," he said. Then Bakhit wrapped it carefully in the cloth and put it away.

As they approached the wadi, Bakhit showed him where he was to gather stones today. Again he would be on his own most of the time, in and out of sight high above the others.

He tucked the hem of his robe up into his belt, then wrapped the loose ends of his kaffiyeh around his head and tucked them in. Dressed now for work, he climbed to his stones. He did not need to search for them. He knew well the many places, high up, where they had already gathered themselves and waited — maybe centuries — till he needed them. Pulling rags from under his belt to tie around his hands, he set to work.

When the sun was halfway to its highest point, he knew he was far enough ahead to rest for a while. He sat down on an open slope where he could be seen from the wadi. When his breathing was easy again and he was sure the guard on duty had noticed him, he stood and turned back into the rocks.

Quickly, he moved away from the wadi, climbing a steep slope behind a protecting ledge, sliding through a narrow opening in the rocks, finally emerging on the side of his own tiny valley. This surprising spot was completely hidden from the wadi on the south and the hostage camp on the northwest, but was approachable from the flatter northeast, from where the old car must once have been driven or towed. He climbed downward until he could see it: the old-fashioned, curvy-fendered green luxury sedan — an ordinary-enough sight in some junkyard back home but an odd one here. A modern dinosaur — a fossil from his own civilization. He shivered. After this he would not make himself look at it again. He had come to say good-bye.

From there he climbed quickly back to his point of entry, where he stopped to eat his orange, and to think. Should he go back to work at once? Or did he dare do what he suddenly wanted to — climb up to see the secret reflector once more? There was plenty of time, and he was sure that by staying to the north face of the peak he could get there again without being seen. Even so, he knew the other hostages wouldn't approve of his going — of his taking even the tiny chance of being seen when the trip wasn't necessary.

A small bird suddenly landed nearby, and for a moment they watched each other. "What are you doing way up here?" he asked. With its serious gleaming eye, it might have been asking him the same thing. "I'm a prisoner," he explained, pleased with his answer because the truth beneath it was that here, alone between the hot white sky and the bare stone, he had come to feel a kind of fierce freedom that was his own strange secret.

The bird flew off, but somehow the moment had helped him decide. He was used to doing whatever others seemed to need him to do — the other hostages, Bakhit, his father and mother. He didn't mind that; he liked it, and he was good at it. But this once he would do something that was for no one in the world but himself.

Now that he had made up his mind, he moved quickly — to the north side of the special peak and upward. He was careful to choose the most sheltered sections, even though he was sure there was no one anywhere below to see him.

From below, this crag looked like all the others. Only from very near the top was it apparent that its upper surface was a shallow indentation, just a few feet long and tilted to the east. Into this space Steven now crawled, keeping his body low. The reflector was just as he had left it: three carefully wedged hubcaps — two inverted to concentrate reflected light rays, one right side up to provide a weaker but more widely visible gleam — and his own secret addition, an oversized side mirror, badly cracked but all still in its frame, which he had found buried in the sand beside the car. Following Gib's instructions, he had angled two of these objects to reflect the late morning sun back eastward, where the people in the little plane might notice; the other two were set to reflect upward, in hopes of a spy satellite. Steven had his doubts about spy satellites, but the little plane was real, and he loved to imagine what it would be like to be riding in it, looking out the window, when it crossed the path of the reflector. A bright wink from the mountain, he thought; that's what the pilot would see.

Pleased that all was still in order, he wiped the nearest hubcap with his loose sleeve to remove any dust. He was careful not to touch the metal with his bare fingers; even lying to the side of it, he could feel the intensity of its heat. Then he slipped down from the secret place and returned to his work.

For another hour or so he moved stones, until he heard Bakhit's whistle calling him to lunch. He hurried to an open point to wave his response, then started down.

From the path he could see the four low walls of rock that now stretched more than halfway across the wadi. It was strange: the hidden reflector was the greatest accomplishment of his life — a dangerous, important feat he had managed all on his own; yet at this moment he felt even greater pride in those dikes. He had worked on them as hard as anyone on his team, and the men had relied on him as on each other. Looking down at the dikes, he was swept with a sudden longing for his parents to see them. For them to stand where he was walking now, holding each other's hand, looking with amazement at what their son had helped to build.

He slowed his pace, stricken; this wish-picture of his parents brought a wave of pain. Lately he'd promised himself that he would keep his mind in the present as much as possible; that he would think of his mother, when he needed to, or of his father, but not of both of them together. Not even of the three of them together, anymore. Once he had known just how to do that with a magic intensity that might keep the family safe, but he had lost the feel of it.

Below, his teammates were spreading out the meal. Bakhit looked up for Steven and waved him on, his raised hands saying, *Come and see, we have something special today.*

Steven moved more quickly again, exploding the inner picture of his parents by an act of will. Darn them anyway, he thought. They've got to take care of themselves. I have my own work to do.

When Steven got back to the hut at the end of the workday, he learned what had been happening there. The statement had been submitted to Assad, who had left at once by truck to deliver it to the za'im and the council of advisers. They would have to wait several days till he could return with the official response.

Martha was sick. Her glumness of the morning had developed into a real stomach upset. She had practically worn a path in the rock, going to the latrine. Steven shouldn't *mention* food to her; even the idea of it made her feel worse. Fuad had agreed to let the rest of them eat outside the hut tonight, so the smell of supper wouldn't bother her.

"How are things in the wadi?" asked Gib.

Steven suddenly realized how long it had been since Gib had been there. "Good. The dikes look great. Maybe your foot will be okay so you can go see them soon."

Gib twisted his mouth into an odd expression. "I'll settle for seeing National Airport," he said finally. "Thanks anyway."

Eighteen

By bedtime Martha was too sick even to get to the latrine. Jessica cared for her behind the curtain as well as she could. During the night Matt could hear them murmuring; he himself slept fitfully.

He turned again and again on his mat, the phrases of the statement swirling crazily through his thoughts. It was a preposterous statement, remembered this way, in the sleepless dark; but what filled him half with excitement, half with dread was that by day he believed in it, in every word of it. Without ever quite deciding to do so, he had argued each point until he agreed with it. Now, if and when he got to deliver the statement, he would have to defend it — not as a pretense he could drop when the others were safe, but as something he had come to believe in. The awful thing was imagining how happy, welcoming faces might freeze as they heard him say, yes, the statement was their own work; yes, he himself believed in it. One hundred percent. Unilateral nuclear disarmament. And his father's face? What would he see there?

The next day Martha was no better. It was Friday, so everyone had to sit in the hut all day. It seemed to Matt the longest day yet, and the most unreal: his preoccupation with the statement was shattered by the increasing worry about Martha. Jessica reported that she was feverish and shaking and could seldom keep down even a swallow of water. Fuad said nothing could be done until Assad's return. Jessica asked him to call Assad on the radio; he said that was not possible.

That night Martha moaned steadily in her sleep, and no one else slept much at all. In the morning they pleaded with Fuad, but he was adamant. "Assad decide. Assad come today. Go now to wadi."

It was a relief to have work to do. When the day was over, Matt hurried back ahead of the others, craving good news: that Assad was back, that the za'im agreed to send Matt with the statement, that Martha was better. He burst into the hut.

"She's delirious," said Gib. "She's burning up."

Jessica's face was white and angry. "Fuad refuses to do a thing except have the guards get our water, so I can stay with her. I keep putting wet rags over her to try to bring the fever down, but it isn't helping."

"You know what Mustapha wants to do?" Gib's lips were tight. "He wants Fuad to bring in some Beduin who will cure her by making cuts on her back. He showed me *his* scars."

"Oh, God." Matt turned to the window. "Assad, come fast."

But Assad did not come. Through the night they waited, hearing Martha's moaning change into frenzied, senseless talk that Jessica tried to answer until she gave up and began to sob.

The next morning Matt sent Sidney and Steven to the wadi but refused to go himself. To his surprise, Fuad did not protest. "Fuad," said Gib through clamped teeth, "she's dying!"

Fuad shook his head. "If Allah wills," he said.

Jessica had had almost no sleep for forty-eight hours, and now Matt and Gib insisted on relieving her. Matt moved Martha into their area by gently dragging out her mat as she slept on it. Now the brothers could take over the chores of rewetting the cloths draped over her arms and legs and easing drops of water into her mouth. Beyond the curtain, Jessica slept at last.

The boys sat in silence, moving only to wet the cloths from time to time. Martha's round face had oddly sunken cheeks now, and her limp arms and legs seemed no longer pudgy. Matt watched how her fingers sometimes moved in her fevered sleep. Of all of them, she had been the toughest. It was unthinkable that they could manage without her childish courage, her energy.

Gib stirred, carefully moving his foot to a new position. Matt thought suddenly: that foot should be getting better by now. Maybe something broke and is healing wrong.

On the wall behind Gib, Adam's hand still reached for the trowel, and God's own hand still reached toward Adam's — reaching, but not quite touching. Damn it, thought Matt, I am so tired of waiting. Our hearts will collapse from waiting. Implode. The rest of us will die of imploded hearts, even before Martha dies.

After a while the boys reached out at the same moment to change the cloths. We are not brothers for nothing, Matt thought.

They were sitting at supper — again in front of the hut — when they heard the truck. They jumped to their feet. Matt covered his heart, shocked by its sudden violence. Assad called out in excitement as he approached. "It is acceptable! Your statement is acceptable. It is already on the way to the States."

Matt's mind froze. "What about me?"

Assad's eyebrows moved to an odd position. "The council did not agree to that idea. The statement goes alone."

Matt could not answer, could not even adjust his face to hide the shock.

"You should be grateful." Assad went on. "At least your statement goes. The za'im wants to see what your father will do."

"The za'im may be disappointed," said Gib grimly. "We told you he ought to send Matt."

From a distant orbit of shock and despair, Matt watched as Jessica almost pulled Assad into the hut where Martha lay, breathing with a rasping noise as she slept. He crouched to look at her.

"It's something terrible." Jessica's voice shook. "She's been like this three days, and Fuad won't do anything. You must get on the radio and get a doctor with medicine here, at once. A *real* doctor."

"Maybe in a few days she'll be better."

"No! Tomorrow she may be dead." Gib limped in behind them. "She's gotten worse every day, and she's burning with fever. She's dying, Assad. How will *that* look in the world papers?" The words were thick with anger. Assad straightened to look at him. "You're so proud of how Islam protects women. Is this how you do it? Who will listen to your big ideas when they know you let a little girl die without doing a thing to help her?"

Assad stared at him, crouched again to look at her, then left the room. They watched him break into a run toward the other hut.

"Oh, thank God," said Jessica. "He's going to his radio."

"But the rescue plan!" Sidney's voice, for the first time since the kidnaping, quivered like a child's. Imploding hearts, thought Matt. We will die of that.

"Later," said Gib. "We'll think about that later."

They were still watching when Assad burst out of his hut and ran back toward theirs, shouting to the guards.

"Is a doctor coming?" asked Jessica, as he approached.

196

"No. She will go to a hospital. Fold her blanket to put under her. We will bring the truck as close as possible." Other men were gathering now, and he ran to meet them.

"Oh, thank heavens!" Jessica turned to go for the blanket.

"Wait!" whispered Sidney. His urgency stopped her. "A hospital! Did you ever hear of a terrorist hospital?" They stared at each other, eyes wide.

"Jessica, quick," said Gib. "Get your map. Oh, Lord, if we'd known, we could have written down some other stuff, too."

Matt grabbed Gib's arm. "What if the hospital isn't friendly, and they realize we've smuggled out the drawing?"

Gib shook his head. "We'll have to take the chance."

"But Assad and the guards, or whoever drives her. It'll be awful if *they* find it. It'll be the end of everything."

"Hurry up!" Sidney jumped to the window. "I hear the truck."

With the drawing in hand, Jessica dropped to her knees beside Martha. "Thank God for Muslim modesty. None of them would dare check her underwear. Turn around and watch the door, you guys."

Matt carried Martha to the truck; Matt and Sadik laid her on the narrow bench in the back of the cab. With Sadik at the wheel and Assad beside him, the truck turned around and jolted away.

"The bumps alone could kill her," gasped Jessica.

"Where are they taking her?" asked Steven. "I mean, where's a hospital, out here?"

Gib's face looked grim. "A long way away, I imagine."

They stood watching the truck curve out of sight until Fuad approached, waving them back into the hut. Steven put his fists tight against his mouth and whispered into them. Jessica put a hand on his shoulder. No one asked him what he was saying.

Nineteen

Assad was gone for more than two days. He came back tired, angry, and wild-eyed, and would tell them nothing about Martha. "When your government responds well to the new messages we have sent, then I will tell you what we have done with your friend."

Tense and irritable himself, Gib risked a complaint. "If you'd sent Matt along, the statement would have had a better chance —"

"Quiet! You will not criticize the za'im. Do you ask to be punished? We will speak no more today." He left in a swirl of air, and after that he seldom visited their hut. It seemed to Matt that he spent more time than usual inside his own.

"I'll bet he's in there on the radio a lot these days," Gib mused aloud on the third evening after Assad's return. "I wonder if things are going badly for them. He's not just bad-tempered; I think he's scared. The others seem nervous, too. Even Mustapha. That's got to mean something."

"Maybe it means Martha's dead," muttered Sidney grimly.

"Don't say that," Jessica murmured. "Don't even think it."

"It might be true."

"Don't think it anyway." There was a tremor in Jessica's

voice that Matt had never heard before. "How long can we take this, you guys? It was better when we were working on the escape plan, or writing the statement. But now there's nothing left to do, and with Martha gone . . ." She leaned her forehead against the knuckles of one hand. Matt could see her closed eyelids quiver. "It seems like a big ax fell out of nowhere and chopped her away. Now at night I lie and wonder where it's going to fall next."

"Come on. Everyone's so uptight," said Sidney. "Except maybe —" He pointed a thumb toward Steven, who knelt at the window, tuned out from their conversation, resting his head in the crook of an elbow as he watched the darkening sky.

Gib was sitting next to Jessica. Now he turned to her and casually put a hand on her foot, as though that much comfort might help her hear what he was going to say. Watching, Matt wished that it were his own hand. "Listen, Jess," Gib said. "Everybody. Don't forget, we got some of our clues out of here, after all. If it's a real hospital they took Martha to, things should be humming already. She can tell people a lot of things — like about the reflector and the French plane. Even if she's too sick or something, at least they'll have the map. *Somebody* ought to figure out who she is, and what it means. So just hang on, okay?"

Jessica's shoulders relaxed a little, and her head fell back against the wall. The tips of her fingers held her eyelids shut, but Matt could see wetness pooling under them.

Her tears could always make the others miserable. Sidney squirmed and turned away, toward Steven. "Hey, Steven," he said. "What are you watching for, man? Think the scenery's gonna change?"

Steven shook his head dreamily. "Just listening."

"What for?"

After a pause: "Sometimes Bakhit whistles good night to me."

"What? Wow, Steve. You sure have an imagination."

Again the unhurried shaking of the younger boy's head. "I'm a good listener, though."

The next day, as usual, Matt and Sidney and Steven worked at the wadi. Afterward, when they gathered around the low table for supper, Sidney sat fidgeting with his spoon until Mustapha had left them. His glowing eyes were eloquent.

"What's up?" asked Gib.

"I saw the little French plane today."

"So?"

"So today's Sunday. It doesn't usually fly on Sunday."

Spoons paused in midmotion. Then, afraid of too much hope, Matt dipped his again. "Maybe it just had an extra flight."

"Maybe. But it was closer, too. Not a lot — but closer."

Steven's eyes widened. "Maybe they've seen it! The wink from the mountain!"

Gib was yielding to the excitement. "Did the guards around you notice it?"

"I don't think so. You can't often hear it, you know; the wind's blowing the wrong way. So it's easy to miss."

"Good. Now, if it happens again, we sure don't want the guards to notice. So don't any of you look at it. Don't look *for* it, either. Jessica and I can watch for it from here. It'll be good to have something to do." He glanced at Jessica, and Matt watched their two faces shine with the same warm hope.

Or perhaps it was not just hope. Perhaps there was something else in both their faces. He realized for the first time — how could he have overlooked it till this moment? — what it might mean that now Jessica and Gib were alone in the hut together for much of each day. At the least, they had hours to talk privately. And if that secret look meant something special was growing between them, then the hand that had touched her foot so casually last night might have already had other experiences of touching her, holding her.

He concentrated on the soup, but what he tasted instead was his own exclusion from something lovely and hidden that seemed suddenly to have bloomed in this dusty, forsaken place.

For almost another week, they hung on. To Matt it seemed as though the fingers of their minds had frozen in a desperate grip on the two thoughts that might keep them from falling into nothingness — Martha and the little French plane. And the plane seemed to reward them; late in the week it flew a second extra journey. That evening the hut hummed with revived hopes.

Except for Gib. Full of encouragement just a few days before, he seemed to Matt oddly silent now, sitting with his head back against the wall, studying his hands. When Steven spied a big lizard outside and Jessica and Sidney joined him at the window to argue about it, Matt crawled over for a private moment with his brother. "Gib. What's the matter?"

"Ah-h-h." Pent-up breath was released in a whispered sigh. "I can't think what to do."

"About what?"

"I'm afraid they're going to move us."

"What?"

"It's been different ever since Assad got back. You don't see it so much because you're gone all day. More conversations in his hut with Fuad. A lot more coming and going of guards. This morning I even saw Umar. Assad seemed to be giving him instructions, and then I heard him go start some kind of work on the truck."

"Why would they move us?" A thought chilled him. "Martha?"

"That's why I'm afraid. Maybe they think she can tell people too much."

Matt dropped his head back. "Oh, God, please, no. Then all the clues, the reflector . . ." He couldn't finish.

"You got it. I sure as hell hope I'm wrong. But — you watch tomorrow. See what you notice."

What Matt noticed the next day, his heart sinking, was that the crews at the wadi were half their usual size. "I couldn't ask why, and no one gave me a clue," he whispered miserably to Gib after supper. "But look, let's still not say anything to the others. Not yet. I couldn't bear it."

"Me either. Anyway, we're not sure. Not yet."

That night they again lay side by side, wakeful. How many nights had Matt lain like this, hating this miserable room, staring at the rectangular shapes of faint light that were the windows? Yet now he was sweating with fear that very soon they might be taken from this place — only to be hidden somewhere else, some place infinitely worse because it would again be utterly unknown.

He thought he wouldn't sleep at all. But then someone was urgently shaking his knee, and he opened his eyes to the gray predawn. Gib knelt close to him. His whisper was soft as breathing. "Come look."

Crouching together at the front window, they raised their heads just high enough to see out. In the usual place on the opposite slope the Arabs were beginning their morning prayers, their spread rugs making neat patches of dark against the gray stone. Much nearer, the guards on duty at the main post· had spread their own rugs there, their rifles lying beside them. The soft chanting, the bowing, rising, prostrating began.

So every morning started. Why had Gib gotten him up for it this time? Matt frowned at him questioningly.

"Keep watching."

Suddenly, beyond the kneeling guards now touching their foreheads to the ground, two strange Arabs in gray robes appeared for just an instant as they dashed from behind a boulder to the cover of Assad's hut. At the same moment Matt jumped at a soft noise that was much closer: something was brushing against the windowless wall of their own hut, moving toward the front. In the next moment there was a shouted command, and from hiding places in front and to the right of them rushed more gray-robed strangers with rifles raised. Incredibly, they were wearing combat boots. Matt grabbed Gib's arm, flooded with hope.

From the front row of worshipers Assad leaped to his feet, snatching up his rifle and barking an order, but there was a burst of gunfire and he fell. Matt gasped. There were more shouts, more shots, and inside the hut cries of alarm as the other hostages woke. At that moment the bar on the door scraped loudly, the door itself flew open, and the five prisoners stared into the face of a big man dressed in a gray robe and kaffiyeh like the others — but a *black* face with thick features, which turned Matt's stomach upside down with joy: an American face.

"Hey. Everybody all right? We've come to take you home."

They flew into his arms.

"It's okay, now. It's gonna be okay. Five of you? Great. Everybody down and over into that corner. Quick! Stay low."

They followed his gesture, scrambling into the front corner and huddling there. The oldest three began to sob with relief. Steven stared at them, his eyes so round with surprise that Gib laughed through his tears. Matt was choking on his.

"It's okay, Stevie. It's great. We're happy. Just keep breathing, man."

Three other Americans carrying machine guns dashed into the hut and took positions at the windows. They've practiced all of this, Matt thought, watching them. His eyes were still swimming — now with gratitude. The black officer raised his hand for quiet. Matt held his breath. Nearby there were only the calls of the American team; coordinating efforts as the Arabs were rounded up. But back toward the tents there was still a commotion: shouting in English, then in Arabic — Khaled's voice, he thought. Rifle fire, from several places, and then the deadly chatter of a machine gun. Finally silence. One of the men at the windows glanced across at them and winked broadly.

Once they all jumped at the sudden sound of distant smashing, but the leader nodded reassuringly and pointed toward the other hut. Assad's radio equipment, that would be. Several times they heard steps running past, and twice the sounds of small groups returning. "I bet they got 'em all," Sidney whispered.

Suddenly there was the harsh, familiar burst of an engine starting. "The truck . . ." Matt was up on his knees, frightened without knowing why. The officer shouted out the door, his voice lost in the growing roar of the engine, and then in staccato rifle fire. Kneeling, Matt watched through the front window as Assad's truck hurtled suddenly into view, racing toward a group of Americans moving a wounded man, who pushed each other out of the way just in time. As it passed, the black officer barked and the man at the window opened fire. In that instant Matt saw over the man's head that the driver was Umar. Now he heard machine-gun fire from outside, but still no change in the truck's wild roar, just frantic bouncing as it hit rougher ground until there was suddenly an awful pause — followed by a terrible series of crashes. From deeper and deeper into the ravine.

There was a moment of stunned silence. The man facing the ravine whistled softly at what he had seen. Matt slumped to the floor, shaking. "He was the hater," he said finally, looking up at the black man. "Umar. He was the only one who hated us. And we never had a chance to know why."

A new American burst into the room. Under the Arab kaffiyeh, his bushy red eyebrows looked incongruous. "We account for twenty-two of them. Plus that one who just took the dive. How many do you kids figure there should be, total?"

"That's about right," Gib answered.

"Okay, good. Then we'll get out of here, before we learn different. You're Gib, right? You get carried, on account of your foot. Everybody else can run? Good. If you've got shoes, get 'em on right away. We'll be getting the sign any minute."

They scrambled for shoes and their few belongings — jackets, the little stones they had used for games. Matt saw Sidney grab the denim yarmulke he had kept rolled in his mat.

The black officer gestured to the door, where two men held a canvas litter. "Gib, here's your taxi. Easy does it."

"A stretcher? Hey, I can walk."

"Not fast enough. Up you go, now, quick."

Stepping out of the hut behind his brother, Matt caught his breath. Most of their former captors stood under guard, their hands at this moment being tied behind them. But four bodies sprawled motionless on the ground, their rifles lying beside them like broken-off limbs. Matt could see the faces of two of them: Bakhit and, yes, Assad turned ghastly, bloodied chests to the sky. Beyond them, the Americans were lifting two of their own onto litters — one who moved his head steadily from side to side, in pain, and one who did not move at all.

Stricken, Matt dropped his eyes from the sight.

What he was now looking at seemed terrible enough: three rows of intricately crafted prayer rugs, curiously vacant on the grim stretch of rock, abandoned in the pattern of prayer.

Now all of the hostages were out of the hut, staring. Behind Matt, Jessica's gasp was like a sob. "Oh, they were *praying!*"

From the litter, Gib reached for her wrist. "Jessica, for God's sake —" She covered her mouth with her free hand.

"Easy, kids," said the big black man soothingly, taking Steven's hand. "Follow those stretchers. The men who'll run beside you will help you if you need it. We don't have too far to go."

For a moment they looked across at the group of defeated guards. "Allahu akbar!" Fuad called out to them, his face impassive.

"Amen," Jessica called back. Then the stretchers began to move, and they all turned away.

But now they were approaching the sprawled bodies. Matt, running behind the black man and Steven, saw the younger boy suddenly pull toward them. "Oh, no, is that Bakhit? Stop, please — is that Bakhit?" Without breaking stride the officer swung Steven up into his arms and turned the boy's face into his shoulder. "Come on, my man. Can't stop now. We're goin' home." He kept Steven's eyes firmly shuttered with his big hand till they were well over the ridge and out of sight.

The escape route led them past Assad's hut and eastward, toward the well. The man with bushy eyebrows traveled beside Matt, a rifle in one hand and a walkie-talkie in the other.

They ran, walked to rest, ran again. Higher on the rocks on either side of the main group Matt could see scouts.

Behind them, the last of the liberators came into view at a run, their heavy boots noisy on the rock. Matt glanced back. "What did they do with *them*?" he asked his companion.

"Locked 'em up in your little house. Till someone comes along and lets 'em out. Or till they free each other's hands and dig a hole through the wall. Their turn to sweat, right?"

The group again slowed to a walk. Bushy Eyebrows kept up a steady scanning of the bluffs in all directions while his walkie-talkie crackled into his ear. "Think they have any reinforcements anywhere?" he asked Matt. "Another camp nearby, or anything?"

Matt shook his head. "No idea where their headquarters is." He had to gasp for breath. "Far as we could tell, these guys were really alone here, hiding out from everyone. We think even the local tribe doesn't know what's going on."

His companion shook his head in amazement. "Incredible. Nearly two months to find out where the hell you are — and then a piece of cake. Sitting ducks. What a piece of cake." But he never stopped his continuous search of the horizon.

"Martha!" Matt had forgotten. "Do you know anything about Martha Stediman?"

The long face turned to grin at him, rusty eyebrows high. "The whole world does! She's safe in Germany, doing fine. The secret part is that she's been talking her head off. How do you think we found out where you were? Then we spotted your signal and followed your map right in."

They turned abruptly south, descending from the ridge across a slope of loose gravel and then winding through a narrow gorge. Suddenly they rounded a last hump of rock and emerged onto flatland, which stretched to the east. The sun rising opposite them glinted on the windshields of several oversized Jeep-like vehicles, painted the color of sand and equipped with huge tires.

"Let me off this thing." Gib was up on his elbow on the stretcher. "Lying down is no way to go home."

"Is this really happening?" said Jessica, looking around at their rescuers. "Can I really start believing it?"

Another officer opened the doors of the nearest vehicle. With his arms raised, the loose sleeves of his robe fell back, and they could see the fitted sleeves of his uniform. "Okay, three of you in this one, two in that one. Quick now."

"Where are the helicopters?" asked Sidney, stretching to take the big step up.

"That's the next part of the trip." The officer gave him a boost. "We have to get there, first."

The black officer led Matt and Steven to the second vehicle. Throughout the ride eastward into the rising sun, Steven sat on the big man's lap, clinging to him tightly and crying into his chest. The man whose face had signaled their liberation stroked the boy's back and murmured to him, winking at Matt reassuringly over his head, as though this was what his entire elite rescue training had prepared him for — this hour of sitting in strange, flowing clothes, hugging a newly rescued child who could only sob as though his heart would break.

Twenty

     S o you may feel pretty strange, for a while," the young
doctor concluded. His eyes were so earnest that Matt found
it hard to keep looking at them. "And this evening, when you
meet your parents at Wiesbaden, *their* feelings may kind of
overwhelm you. Just remember that weird feelings are okay;
they're natural after what you've been through, and they're
not going to last."

He was sitting on the arm of a seat in front of them, scanning their faces once more. Finally he stood up. "I'll lay off
the lectures for a while. But come on up, anyone, if you'd
like to talk — to me, or to any of us."

A flight attendant started toward them to ask, for the tenth
time, if they needed anything, but the doctor waved her away.

It was odd, Matt thought: with half of the special plane to
spread out in, they had instinctively huddled together. Sidney and Steven, in window seats, turned to look down again
toward the whitecaps of the Mediterranean far beneath them.
Steven was still hugging the plastic bag that held his Arab
clothing.

That was the one thing that was very different about them
now: their new clothes, so peculiar after two months of Bed-

uin thobes. The change had made them a little shy with each other.

Matt glanced across the aisle at Gib, in cords and a turtleneck, and beyond him at Jessica, in a new fall skirt and sweater. Whatever specialness had been growing between the two of them would be seriously threatened by this return to their own lives. Well, that would be all right with *him*.

Suddenly he needed space. He moved forward a couple of rows, flopping down into a window seat. Far below, the Mediterranean was a vastness like the vastness of rock he had left behind.

Why this sensation of being so much alone? Just because of Gib and Jessica? He leaned back, concentrating on it. No. It was because his feelings about the coming reunion were far more complex than theirs. Actually, this seemed like only half of his homecoming, the second half; he had already sent a part of himself on ahead, in the statement. By now millions of Americans who had never met Matt Vereen had read something that bared a lot of his mind and heart, and he was afraid of their reaction.

Looking down at the distant sea, he thought once more through the points of the statement and found none from which he was willing to retreat. Instead, he was going to have to fight for them. What would people think?

Worst of all, what would his father think? *I'm coming home changed, Dad. You liked what I was. Will you want what you're getting back?*

The answer would be terribly important. Gib had been right, after all: how steadily Matt had labored for the attention, the approval of his father!

But now there were things that mattered even more. How could he ever explain what had happened to him? He was like one of those astronauts who'd been shot thousands of miles into space and then returned with a permanently different view of life.

Matt turned his head restlessly, tired of the unaccustomed pain. He should concentrate on the present, on this flight to freedom. The cream-colored panels at the front of the cabin had an interesting design — a strangely familiar pattern of maroon rectangles. He would concentrate on them.

But in a minute Gib arrived, leaning heavily on seat backs as he moved, and dropped into the seat beside him. "What's up, man? Here we are, finally safe and going home — and you're by yourself, looking terrible. What's eating you?"

Matt blew out his breath heavily. "The statement. I'm going to stand by it. And I don't look forward to getting clobbered."

Gib shook his head. "You're really asking for it, aren't you? Matt, the statement could never get anywhere. Even if everything in it was right. Americans would never agree to unilateral nuclear disarmament. That would take a miracle."

Matt stirred restlessly. "We got ourselves rescued, didn't we? I'd have said *that* would be a miracle. But it wasn't. It was a hell of a lot of guts and good thinking. And you were the one who said we had to do it! Accept responsibility for our own survival. I didn't want to believe we had to — but you forced me to. Now I guess I do believe in that kind of responsibility, damn it. And maybe that kind of miracle. And it's going to cost me."

For a while they both were quiet. Matt gazed again at the maroon rectangles at the front of the cabin, letting his eyes go out of focus so there were twice as many of them. Finally Gib sighed. "You are nuts. You know we can't work with you on this. Well, maybe Jess, but nobody else. All *I'll* do for you is apologize. I've always thought you were just on your own personal ego trip with Dad. I take back what I said. I

211

will no longer think of you as kissing up to Dad." He grinned. "As flying kamikaze, maybe. But not as kissing up."

Matt twisted his mouth ruefully. "Maybe you weren't totally wrong."

"Well." Gib stood to go.

"Hey," said Matt. "Thanks for coming up here."

Gib shrugged one shoulder. "Jessica made me."

"Well, thanks to Jessica."

Suddenly tired, he leaned back again, gazing at the maroon rectangles through half-shut eyes. Under the fringe of his lashes, the dark shapes wavered, seemed to float free of the panels they were painted on. Why did they disturb him so?

His eyes focused with a shock as he remembered. The Muslim prayer rugs, laid out for worship, so suddenly abandoned. How spooky they would look from a helicopter — spread out like some urgent but untranslated message, under the desert sky. And who was there to decode that message, to deliver it, if not he himself?

He was no longer young; he was old. The sight of those prayer rugs was burned into the front of his skull forever.

Only gradually did he notice the approach of a broadly smiling young member of the flight crew. The fellow had spoken to them before, and something in his manner had already put them off. "That guy looks like an ad for teeth," Sidney muttered now.

He perched on the arm of a seat, tugging at the creases in his slacks to loosen them. "Well, how you doin'? Everybody okay?"

They nodded.

"Well, you're going to have the life of Riley now, aren't you? Guess they'll keep the crowds and the reporters away from you as long as they can. They'll stuff you with hamburgers, french fries, milkshakes. Things you've been missing. Right?"

"Right," growled Gib, frowning.

"Why will they keep people away?" asked Steven.

"So you won't have to keep telling about the bad things the terrorists did to you, stuff like that," their guest volunteered.

"Oh," said Steven, looking away and hugging his bundle.

"Or answer questions about that statement thing. Gee, those bastards must have really leaned on you to get you to write a thing like that."

They stared at him, speechless. He looked from face to face, his smile beginning to fade into uncertainty. From the front of the cabin, the doctor had been watching; now he got up and started toward them. The visitor rose. "Heck, don't worry about it. People know you were under horrible pressure. They won't take that thing seriously. After all, you're just kids." The doctor met him in the aisle, and they spoke briefly.

"Geez," said Sidney finally. "I think we were just mugged."

"Maybe that wasn't anything," said Jessica. "Maybe we're really oversensitive. A hostage phenomenon, or something."

"Oh, no." Gib's growl deepened. "A vacation in the rocks doesn't mean you can't still recognize a meathead when you see one."

Matt turned to gaze out the window. So he'd been right; confrontations over the statement wouldn't be long in coming. For the first time he felt a stir of excitement at the prospect.

Matt moved forward to the top of the metal stairway, blinking into the dark, holding Steven's hand. Ahead of him, crew members were helping Gib down the steps toward the cluster of officials waiting below. Under lights beyond a police barricade a group of people were cheering; in front of them stood the parents. Suddenly Matt could see his father and mother, their faces white in the sharp light. They were waving and waving. His own arm shot high, and his sight blurred.

He and Steven started down the steps, moving slowly because of Gib. "Matt," said the younger boy, staring down at the step in front of him. "See that lady over at the right? She's got real long hair and a yellow coat. She's my mom."

"Yeah, I see her. She's waving at you! Wave back."

"Just tell me. Is my dad with her? Tall, with glasses. Look all around."

"Mm — no, I think she's alone. Come on, Stevie, wave!" But it was several more slow steps before the boy lifted his head, and then his hand.

In a moment the two groups were in each other's arms. Matt's father held him fiercely, without moving or speaking, until Gib said, "I'll have some of that, please."

Matt turned to his mother, who was laughing through her tears. "Oh, wow," he said into her wind-blown hair. "Is this real?"

Slowly, the reunited families moved toward a waiting bus. ". . . a little reception, now," Matt's mother was saying. "Oh, Martha's frantic to see you, but the doctors say not till tomorrow. And Matt, Ernesto is coming tomorrow. Remember him? That nice old man has been praying for you every day. At the Arch of Titus in the Forum, for some reason. They're flying him up here for a few days . . ."

". . . a specialist who'll look at your foot tomorrow." His father was half-supporting Gib as they walked. "These days they can do practically anything with bones. Sure you don't want to use the crutches, for now?"

What about the others? Matt looked for them. The three

Goodmans were walking just ahead of the Vereens, their arms linked. Sidney's father's voice boomed: ". . . special prayers in the service, and everything. If you want, we could even call him up tomorrow, to set a new date. Listen, though, that'll be *one* day you'd better not wear your new Arab jewelry!" Their three voices rose in the explosive laughter of relief.

Farther away, Jessica walked with her mother, matching step for step. Well, Matt thought, at least there would be benefits for him if Jessica and Gib stayed special to each other; she was his most committed ally in support of the statement, and her mother might be another . . .

His own mother was looking sideways at him with a teasing quirk to her mouth. "You aren't listening, are you?"

He turned to her sheepishly. "Oh, I'm sorry —"

"That's all right." She tightened the arm around his waist, laughing. "That's typical. Now I know you're really home!"

And Steven? Behind Matt, where the child and his mother were walking, there was only the sound of footsteps for a while. Then he could hear conversation again. "Honey, I have to explain about Dad."

"That's okay." Steven's voice. "You don't need to."

"Actually, he didn't come over here. But he's real eager to see you, and you're going to visit him as soon as we get home."

"Okay."

"What I have to explain to you is hard to say. It's not about you, it's about Dad and me —"

"You don't have to say."

"What?"

"I understand already. You don't have to say."

Inside the bus, Matt's father took the seat beside him. As they began to move, the interior lights went out. Good; it would be easier to talk in the dark. "I sent you a letter," Matt said.

His father was looking at him. "I got it. So did the whole world, actually. You should see the coverage and the reactions you're getting. Especially abroad."

"It said some way-out stuff, but I can't find anything now that I disagree with. I don't think the world is going to disarm unless the U.S. leads the way. What do you think of the statement?"

"I think it's courageous and well argued. The press is very eager to see what I'm going to do about it."

A pause. "What *are* you going to do about it?"

His father chuckled. "Hey, you just got home! You six are the folks with the story to tell." He sobered. "I'm not sure. I'm going to take some risks. You'll be around while I work it out."

Matt must say it now; he must take his own risks. "If it isn't good enough, I'll have to say so. And support someone else. I learned to think for myself out there, Dad. I had to."

A silence between them, a distance. The silence of two adults, negotiating.

"Fair enough. But — I'll try to keep your support." A change in his father's voice now. "I've always thought we'd make quite a team."

Matt drew a deeper breath. The tightness in his chest was easing. "The Muslims have this fascinating thing about Adam. They say God respected Adam, even though he'd been disobedient, because he alone of all the Creation accepted the responsibility of knowledge. I keep thinking about that."

After a moment his father said, "Sounds as though you've got a heck of a story to tell. So far, it's not quite what I'd expected."

"Oh, some of it's pretty strange, all right. Do you know, you had a *fan* out there? There's this guy — you won't believe — this guy in charge of us . . ." But now images had begun to whirl through his head. He suddenly saw not only Assad's arrogant face, but Fuad's dignified one, then Mustapha, proud of himself for bringing the radio, then Assad and the others — Americans, too — sprawled in the predawn . . . "Look, later, okay?"

His father was studying his face. "Right. They told us you shouldn't try to go too fast. You're safe now, that's the main thing. Everyone's safe."

No, he thought. Nobody's safe. But he dropped his head back and shut his eyes to wait for the whirling to pass.

The bus stopped outside a massive building where brightly lighted windows waited to welcome them. His father stood up in the aisle. "Party time. You up to some chow?"

Matt nodded. "Yeah — sure."

Outside the bus, the group walked slowly. Gib was trying the crutches. Nearby came Steven and his mother, hand in hand. With his free arm, Steven hugged the bag of Beduin clothing tightly.

"Here, let me help you with that," said Martin Vereen, reaching for it.

"No, thanks," said Steven, shying away. "I can carry it."

"Ah. Okay." The senator looked harder at the boy's face, then at Matt, inquiringly.

Matt shook his head. "Some things I can never explain."

There was a sudden flurry of excitement among the people waiting at the door to welcome them. Someone came running down the steps. "The President is on the telephone. He wants to greet the young people. Could one of you come ahead quickly so we don't keep him waiting?"

"Wow! Gib should go," said Sidney.

"No way can I hurry with these things," Gib answered. "Jessica, go. Give the man a break."

"Ooh, Jess. Aren't you scared?" asked Steven.

Jessica tossed back her hair. "Of course not. And what if I was? Steven Mahlon, don't you forget it: after what we've done" — now she was running up the steps toward the door — "we can face up to anything."

Matt heard her call echo back from the wings of the building. "Anything. Anything."

Following the echo, he and the others started up the steps toward the waiting light.